The
Peking Switch

The Peking Switch

James J. Marsh

David McKay Company, Inc.
Ives Washburn, Inc.
New York

THE PEKING SWITCH

COPYRIGHT © 1972 BY JOSEPH R. MARSHALL

LIBRARY OF CONGRESS CATALOG CARD NUMBER: 72-84209
MANUFACTURED IN THE UNITED STATES OF AMERICA

The
Peking Switch

Chapter

1

THE icy air hit like a wall and flipped him head over heels. The turbofan engines of the Soviet Il-62 were screaming in the night like a thousand jackals.

"One," he said to himself, hugging his knees as he tumbled. The stars swept across the black sky. The howling wind buffeted him. He was very high, falling end on end. He saw the moon suddenly and the clouds and then the stars again.

Jumping high without an oxygen bottle, it is important to get into position because you can pass out and spin to death. Counting helps you stay with it.

"Two," he said and, letting go of his knees, he started to straighten his legs.

"Three." The wind tugged at his trousers. He tried to sit up to stop the tumbling, and then he lost his breath.

He saw blackness and gasped, sucking in the cold air. But he was too high. Even as he tried to fill his lungs, he knew that it would be futile. It is not lack of air, but too much nitrogen that puts the blackness behind your eyes. Must not pass out.

"Four," he said.

He gasped again and sat up straighter, arms and legs extended. He was still tumbling on his side. The moon sailed in front of him, and the stars turned.

"Five." He pulled in his right arm and then threw it out again. It slowed the tumbling, the blackness began to recede.

"Six." He almost had it now. Sitting as if in a chair, he was falling backward.

"Seven." This is correct, he thought, falling back first, arms and legs out, head up a little. If you pass out in this position you will fall straight while you are unconscious, and you will come to when you get down far enough.

"Eight." The screaming engines had gone.

"Nine," he counted, and then, "Ten."

He had to roll into a dive so he could see where he was going. He pulled his right arm in, tucked his shoulder, and going over, began to arch his back. The wind froze his face. He put out his arms, elbows cocked, palms down, to stop the roll. Then he bent his knees outward like a frog.

He was floating face down on a cushion of air as thick as water and as soft as down, but he could see only the scattered clouds below tinted silver. Like cotton, they had been stretched too far and torn, leaving gaps of blackness. They rose slowly.

His knees began to shake. They shouldn't be shaking now, he had straightened out.

The clouds were coming more quickly. He was going to go right through one of them. It came shooting up. For an instant there was silver everywhere, then blackness. The air turned icy wet, and he was through the cloud.

The sky was now bright enough to read by. He glanced down at the luminous dial of the altimeter riveted to the top of his chest pack. The needle pointed left. He still had plenty of room.

Far below the earth was shadowed black and gray. A few flat mirrors reflected light. They would be lakes and ponds. Smaller points of light were scattered about the hills.

The Aeroflot pilot had been ordered to keep the Il-62 below altitude. He was supposed to throttle back and flash the jump light over the hills near the city of Westphalia in northern New York State. But the pilot had his problems, too, which was why he had kept climbing. He had to make the drop without alerting the American crew which had come aboard at Ottawa.

The ground was coming slowly. He was headed for a lake shaped like a thumbnail with a broad base. At the far end there was a cluster of lights that would be a village. The rest of the lake was dark. It was a good place to come down. At this time of year there were plenty of fishermen scattered around the lake; a man alone in the woods had a reason to be there.

He was dropping near the right shore of the lake. The trees would be pines. If he aimed for the water near the

3

shore he could be out of the harness before he hit. But the water would be freezing, and the chest pack would make it difficult to swim. Then he would have to build a fire and spend a good part of the night drying out. He would take a chance on the pines instead. It was better to run the risk and stay dry.

He studied the ground. The patch of gray just inland from the shore could be a mountain swamp, or a meadow with a few trees, or it could be the side of a cliff.

The parachute would open automatically when he got down far enough, but since he was coming down over the hills, it would be safer to pull the cord early. He would be over the woods, and no one would see him. He would glide to make the gray patch and hope it was a clearing.

He watched the ground come faster. His face was frozen.

Tucking in his right elbow, he reached across his chest with his right hand. With his right shoulder down, the pilot chute would open in the wind and it would go out fast. He grabbed the metal handle, pulled it down to the side hard, and held it, waiting. The chute was in a sleeve.

Then the harness snatched him upright. He bounced a little, hung, and started swinging rapidly. Taking hold of the risers on each side, he steadied himself.

The howling wind had died, leaving the night soft and quiet and cold. He was swinging gently in the darkness, now; as he surveyed the approaching earth to the left he saw the shining surface of the lake. Beyond it was the gray spot in the forest, now looking more like a mountain swamp or a clearing.

He pulled hard on the right shroud. With its open panel

4

at the rear, the parachute was steerable. It turned slowly and slid inland. He had to cross more than a hundred meters of forest. He pulled down on the forward risers, set the drift, and let go.

For a few seconds he glided, and then the trees were reaching up for him. He was not sure that he could make it. He would have to move fast, cross his legs, put his arms over his face.

As he slid over the last trees, he grabbed the rear shrouds, spilling wind and stopping himself. Then he reached for the risers and held himself up to absorb the landing.

The black meadow floor shot up to meet him.

He hit turning and let himself fall, legs and side and butt. Then he was up again, stumbling in the wet clump grass until he caught himself, and stopped. The canopy sank before him. The cloth rustled.

The night was windless, dark, and silent. And the spring smells of wetness and pines were in the air. The clearing stretched perhaps a kilometer, rising in the darkness to join the distant treetops. Behind him, the edge of the forest was a wall.

He had stood a long while, catching his breath, before the owl hooted. It hooted again, and something small ran through the grass. Then the night burst alive with the peeping sounds of tiny creatures who had been scared into silence by his arrival.

Shaking from the cold, he stripped off his gloves, his goggles, and the helmet. He removed the harness, and slipped out of the chest pack, letting them fall to the ground. Bending down, he unbuckled the pack's leather straps, and from the holster stitched to the inside he took a .32 revolver and tucked it into his belt. Then he unstrapped the little folded shovel from the bottom of the pack, set the blade, and stuck it into the ground. The earth was not frozen.

He began to gather up the parachute. It was the only evidence of his arrival which he could not take with him, and so he had to bury it. But the digging would serve to warm him quickly.

It was not yet midnight, he had plenty of time. He would find the edge of the lake and follow it to the cluster of lights, and if the scattered moonlight held, he would be able to move swiftly through the forest.

He wasn't a kid anymore, but he was in good shape. He could walk all night or all day, and he was not due in Westphalia until tomorrow night. He would make it with ease.

Chapter

2

THE Soviet was overdue. Lieutenant James
W. Ligett flew directly over the lake approaching contact,
but his radar picked up nothing. He throttled back and put
the F-105 Thunderchief into a flat turn. The air was still, and
the bright moon, almost full, threw white light on the
clouds below.

He checked flight plan and frequency, and then radioed
them.

"Soviet, this is escort jet zero three niner. How do you
read me?"

"Escort three niner. Soviet reads you clear, over."

"Waiting at contact, Major."

Major Conklin was pilot of the American standby crew
that had boarded the Soviet at Ottawa. The Il-62 was

7

carrying a Soviet disarmament mission from Moscow to Washington. Two Canadian aircraft were escorting it to the U.S. border, where Lieutenant Ligett would take over.

"We're running one zero minutes behind, but on course. We'll be there."

"Roger," he said. He had circled all the way around now, and he, too, was on course.

Edging back on the throttle, he maneuvered the jet into slow turns, first right, then left, sailing squat through the sky. The F-105 flies like a bomb but it stays where you put it, smooth and solid as a rock, and it will do just about anything even in slow flight.

He was in a turn, when Major Conklin reported they were approaching. He rolled the bomb onto its side so he could look below, and then above, and ahead. The radar still showed nothing.

He was about to ask for another position check when he saw the lights blinking red and green far below the banks of clouds. He hit the radio button. "Soviet, escort three niner. Can you give me an altitude?"

"Twelve thousand, climbing slowly. You have us yet?"

"I'll come down and look. I've been waiting at thirty thousand where you filed."

"Sorry, friend." It was another voice, a Canadian. "We're not running this show, you know, but I think I've got you. You're at twelve o'clock. If you come down on degrees two zero zero, you'll pick us up when you come through."

"Righto, Canada."

He kept the bomb turning, straightened out on two hundred degrees, and throttled back. He wanted to let them pull ahead as he went down. He kicked a little right rudder to put the F-105 between two cloud banks. The clouds came up like white hills, and he was under them.

The Soviet was far ahead all lit up, and he could see the lights of the Canadians a little high, port and starboard, tailing her.

He tapped the throttle hard and the bomb jumped, forcing him back against the seat. Control was giving a position check, and by the time they were finished he had caught up.

"Soviet," he said, "escort jet zero three niner on your tail. We'll take over from here, Canada."

"Roger." It was the Canadian's voice. "The way he's going, you've got a slow and low, over."

"A real drag ass," someone said. It was the other Canadian.

"This is Soviet Conklin. Much obliged, Canada, and good luck. Escort three niner starboard and stay well aft until we get up. We're climbing."

"Righto."

Lieutenant Ligett watched the Canadians peel away port and starboard. The Soviet was about a thousand feet below the clouds. He moved the throttle and dropped back. They went up slowly through the mist, and then emerged from the clouds just ahead.

The moonlight turned the Soviet into silver, and illuminated the big red Russian letters on its side. It was still well below speed.

Lieutenant Ligett pulled the throttle back and glanced across the instruments, trusting his eyes to pick out anything wrong. He twisted a little, settling comfortably into his seat.

9

The Soviet was climbing steadily. They had a couple of hours to Washington.

It was minutes later when he saw something drop. It was solid and black and it flashed in the moonlight.

Moving fast, he shoved the throttle and peeled off to starboard. At first he thought it was part of the airplane. He tapped the radio button.

"Major Conklin, this is escort. You dropped something, Major."

"Say again please."

"You dropped something from the aircraft. I'm on it. You have any problems there?"

"Negative on problems. You had better stay with us."

Ligett was coming around in his dive, and he saw it again, below and ahead, turning. It was a man. In the moonlight he could see the legs and arms.

"Escort, everything checks out here."

"I'm on it now," Ligett yelled. "It's a man. But I'm going to lose him in the clouds."

He pulled around tighter. The man was right below him, maybe a thousand feet, falling steadily.

"He's going into the clouds. I can follow him down."

"This is Conklin. Negative. You're flying escort. You had better get back into position."

"You dropped somebody, Major. I can follow him down."

"You come back into position. That's an order, Lieutenant. Do you read me? Over."

Lieutenant Ligett held the jet in a tight spiral dive, watching the man until he disappeared in the clouds. He could have followed him right down to the ground.

"Escort three niner, acknowledge."

They had told him to follow orders, and Major Conklin was in command. "I read you," Lieutenant Ligett said. "Willco and out."

He pulled up into a steep climbing turn, letting the G's glue him into the seat. You can't tear the wings off an F-105.

Soon the bomb was sailing, and the pressure diminished. He edged to starboard, approaching two hundred degrees. The Soviet had been moving right along, still climbing.

He hit the radio button. "Soviet, this is escort three niner moving into position. But you dropped something, Major, you sure as hell dropped something."

"Everything's clean."

"Soviet, this is radar control. We had the unidentified object. We suggest it may have been landing gear."

It had been a man, not landing gear.

Major Conklin came back on the radio. "Soviet captain says the gear checks out. We're moving up to flight plan."

"Maybe you lost a passenger," Ligett said.

"It could have been a piece of gear," the Major said. "Radar control, how do you read on three four point six?"

"Read you clear."

"Are you monitoring?"

"Yes, sir, we've been open all the time. We've got a position on the falling object, and we're notifying proper authorities."

"Thanks, Control," the Major said. "I've got a new ETA Washington. Hours two four three two, over."

"Two four three two, out."

The radio went back on static. That was a little better. At

11

least Control realized the Soviet had dropped something and maybe they knew more than they were letting on. Even if it was only gear, they were in trouble. Lieutenant Ligett had made several dead landings, and one without gear years ago. He still could remember jumping and running before the aircraft stopped. They were spraying foam, but it caught fire anyway. To hell with it. He was just taking orders; it was their problem.

They made Washington right on ETA, and he checked the Soviet's gear. There was nothing missing. Washington gave him a departure heading, and he swung away from the Soviet and over the city.

Minutes later he was on course for home, clear all the way. He flew the needle and let his mind wander. He thought of his wife, Lucy, and the Turners' party. He had drunk too much at the last one, which explained why he'd gotten into the wrestling match on the back lawn. Lucy had been mad as hell. He wouldn't drink that much tomorrow night, he promised himself.

When Ligett called the tower to request landing, they had a message for him.

"Special orders for you," they said. "They want you in Washington."

"Let me have that again," he said.

"We've got a teletype to alert you on arrival, sir. They're cutting orders for you to go to Washington. They want you there by one seven zero zero tomorrow. A Major Rufus Conklin."

"Goddamn it," Ligett said.

"Say again please and acknowledge."

"Thanks. Thanks and willco. I'm approaching on three fifty."

"Cleared for straight in approach."

They were ordering him to Washington tomorrow. Major Conklin would want a report, and he wouldn't get back until late. But there wasn't anything he could do about it. Fly boy, fly boy, fly away home, and he couldn't remember the rest of it.

He rubbed his jaw with the back of his wrist.

He had the field in sight. There was no one else in the sky, and the bomb was going down long and smooth and flat, squatting a little.

His eyes roved across the instruments, across the pale glass and black faces and the rolling numbers. He reached for the lever to drop his landing gear and for a second, in the milky light near the two trembling needles, he saw the figure falling, tumbling in the darkness. Shoving the gear lever into position, he thought, they sure as hell dropped somebody.

Chapter 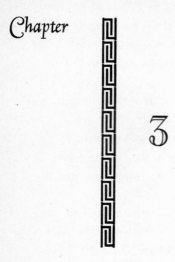 3

"MY name's Hamill," he said. "Albert S. Hamill. I'm expecting a letter, general delivery."

The postman was chewing a toothpick. With his tongue, he moved it to the other side of his mouth. "Hamill," he said as he turned his moon face away from the service window and reached up for a stack of letters. Placing them on the counter, his pudgy fingers began to flip through them.

It was early afternoon, and the Westphalia Post Office was at its busiest. The man who called himself Hamill had been waiting patiently in line for almost ten minutes.

"Hamill," the postman said, plucked a letter, and slid it across the window counter. "There you are." The toothpick was lodged securely in the corner of his mouth.

"Thanks," the man replied.

He took the letter to one of the counters that stood in the center of the lobby, dropped his rucksack onto the floor and studied the white envelope. There was no return address, but the postmark was Westphalia. It had been mailed two days ago, one day before he had climbed aboard the Il-62 in Moscow.

He ripped open the end. There was a piece of yellow cardboard inside but it wouldn't shake out. He ran his finger through the top edge of the envelope and took out the yellow ticket with red lettering. It said, "Municipal Parking, 762 Main Street." There were two other cards as well. A New York State operator's license for Albert S. Hamill, 2168-33 Avenue D, Bronx, New York, and an Avis charge card, also made out to Albert S. Hamill.

With the parking ticket he could get the car. Inside there would be a suitcase packed with clothes. Then he would check in at the Clinton Manor Hotel. They had made a reservation for him in the name of Hamill.

He tucked the cards into his pants pocket and looked up just as the man came through the revolving door. He was fleshy in the face and small, and he wore a felt hat and a double-breasted overcoat. A maroon silk scarf was wrapped around his neck. He was checking the service windows, one after the other.

The man who called himself Hamill stared at him. He thought that he had seen this man before. But it was probably his nerves. He was tired and a little keyed up, and it had been something like twenty years since he had been in this post office. No one in Westphalia knew he would be here on the afternoon of this day.

The man came past him, still examining the service windows. Halfway down the lobby he stepped up to the end of the line before the stamp window.

The man who called himself Hamill picked up his rucksack and went quickly through the revolving door and out into the cold sunlight.

Westphalia's Main Street stretched before him, heavy traffic moving in both directions. Squinting in the bright light, he descended the steps and started toward the parking lot. Even after such a long absence he remembered Main Street: the bus station halfway down the block, the red brick County and City buildings, and the Clinton Manor Hotel.

They had come here every spring to fish, and in the late afternoons, on the way back to the hotel, they always had stopped at the post office. He could remember feeling cold and wet and hungry, his fingers stiff. And he could remember writing postcards, telling his mother how they had caught some brookies and that they were having a good time.

They had always stayed at the Clinton Manor Hotel with its rose-red carpets and small rooms. Every morning his father would get up before dawn and smoke a cigar as he dressed. They would leave the hotel when it was still dark and eat breakfast at a steamy dog wagon, and then they would drive up into the mountains as the sky turned pale blue. They would be fishing by the time the sun rose high enough to make long shadows in the woods.

Before he got the car, he had to make a telephone call. There would be pay telephones in the bus station. He waited for a break in the traffic and quickly crossed the street.

He pushed through the swinging door. A child was crying, and the waiting room was busy. It smelled of cigarette smoke and people. Music played. To his left was a newspaper stand. The telephone booths were against the far wall, the two end booths open and empty.

On his way, he stopped at the newsstand and bought a copy of the *Westphalia News* to make sure that he had enough change for the call. Leaving the door of the booth open, he inserted a dime and dialed Operator. She came on at once. He had almost forgotten how efficient the American telephone system was.

"Operator," he said, "I would like to call New York City 437-6219."

"You can dial that yourself, sir. The code is 212."

"I'm sorry," he said. "How much is it?"

"I'll place the call for you, sir. May I have that number again?"

"New York City 437-6219."

"That will be ninety-five cents for the first three minutes."

"You want me to put it in now?"

"Yes, please, sir."

The coins rang out as they fell. The operator dialed, and the line clicked and hummed and then buzzed intermittently. The telephone was supposed to be manned twenty-four hours a day. He was the only one who had the number, but it could still be tapped. He wasn't supposed to take any chances. He was just letting them know that he had arrived.

"Yes," a voice said.

He shoved the booth door closed with his foot. "Is this New York City 437-6219?"

17

"Yes," the voice said again.

"Could you give me the correct Prague time, please?"

"What?"

"Prague time," he said. "Can you tell me the correct Prague time?"

"Yes," the voice said. "I can give you Moscow time. It is now twenty hundred hours and in two hours it will be twenty-two hundred."

"Two hours?" They wanted a contact in two hours. That was pretty quick. He had been up for two days, moving all night and most of today, and he was bone tired.

"All right," he said.

"Is that all you wanted?"

"Yes," he said. "Thank you for the time." He hung up.

They knew that he was here. In a little while they would use a coin telephone somewhere, a telephone that nobody could have tapped, and they would set up the contact.

He pulled open the booth door. The child was still crying. Across the benches he could see the mother holding him against her shoulder, patting his back to quiet him.

Within an hour he had picked up the car, paid for two days parking and registered at the Clinton Manor Hotel. Although the lobby had been modernized, the corridors still had rose-red carpets, and his room was not much larger than the space the furniture occupied. One window looked out over the town, giving him a clear view across rooftops and down Main Street to the post office.

He put the suitcase on the bed and opened it. There were airline schedules on top of the clothes, United, American, TWA. They were folded thick, red and blue. He was going to have to do a lot of traveling, at least to Colorado and Washington and perhaps the West Coast. He stacked them on the bedside table.

He tossed six shirts—button-downs as he had told them—onto the little dresser, and hung the two suits in the closet. There were socks and shoes, underwear, and ties. The paper bag was full of toilet articles.

Putting the rucksack on the bed beside the suitcase, he began to undress. He tossed the cloth money belt he had been wearing under his shirt over the rucksack.

He went into the bathroom and turned on the bath water. For the few minutes while the bath ran, he puttered around the room in his shorts, putting things away. He left the empty suitcase on top of the bureau.

Bright sunlight was coming through the window.

It would probably be night over there, halfway around the world. The boys would be in bed, and she would be sleeping with the window open. The curtains would be flapping softly if there was any wind.

He went into the bathroom and climbed into the hot bath. He had to relax. Anyway there was no need to be tense now. He sat back in the steaming hot water and closed his eyes. But his mind wandered back to Tu-chan and their sons. And, although from the very beginning he had tried not to think about it, he wondered what they would do if he never made it back.

He got out and dried hard so his skin hurt, and then he shaved. After shaving, he didn't look so tired. He had started to get dressed when the telephone rang.

"Hello," he said.

"Is this room eight twenty-five?" The voice betrayed a slight accent.

"Yes."

"You wanted Moscow time?"

"No," he said, remembering the sequence: Prague, Moscow, Vienna, Paris, London. "Vienna time, if you have it."

"In front of number ten fifty Hamilton Street. It is off Main. In half an hour."

"That's too soon," he said. "I've been moving all day, and I need something to eat."

"It's only a few blocks from you."

"What's the hurry?" he said. "It's dangerous to hurry."

"It has to be tonight."

"I haven't eaten."

"I can give you an hour. Make it seventeen hundred hours local. In front of ten fifty Hamilton Street."

"That's still too soon."

"Are you going to make it?"

"How do I identify you?"

"Follow procedure, and we will find you."

"All right," he said. "All right." But there wasn't any need to rush. He said, "I'll be there."

"Splendid." The line clicked.

He put the telephone back on the cradle and stood for a minute, his hand still on the receiver. He could hear the faint sounds of traffic outside. They were efficient, and they had been waiting for him in Westphalia. Now if he moved right along he would have time to get scrambled eggs or something hot to eat. He dressed quickly.

The suit was just about right except for the waist. Either

the tailor had made a mistake or he had lost a lot of weight in the last two weeks. He pulled the leather belt tighter. The pants fit well enough to wear.

He put on the suitcoat; it fit better. Then he went to the bed where he had tossed the rucksack, opened it and took out the .32. He weighed it in his hand, broke it, spun the cylinder. There was a round in every chamber.

A revolver is bulky and hard to conceal, and they had tried to persuade him to take a Luger or an automatic because they are flat and nestle close against your side or in your pocket. But a revolver never jams, and if you hold it right around the cylinder, it is handier when you don't want to shoot.

He closed the gun and spun the cylinder again. He tucked it under his belt and buttoned the center button of his suit-coat.

He went into the bathroom again and stood back from the sink, looking in the mirror. He had thick eyelashes, a square face and a heavy beard like a Slav, and there were shadows all around the sunken eyes. His hair was still black, but he seemed to stoop more as he got older. He stood straight so he would not look so short. Now he could see his midsection reflected. The gun was not visible. And, wearing a top-coat, he wouldn't have to give it a thought.

Chapter  4

TEN fifty Hamilton Street was a doorway between two stores. He double parked in front of it, following procedure. The door was glass. There was a light behind it, and a short hallway with a staircase leading up to the second floor. There was no one to be seen.

The dress shop to the right of the doorway had closed for the day. A naked mannikin stood in the dark window. On the other side, a gift shop was still doing business. A gold script across the window said, "Notions and Things."

He had been double parked long enough for them to have seen him. He started the engine and drove slowly down Hamilton to Main Street and waited for the traffic light. Then he turned into the traffic and got stuck behind a panel truck. It took him close to five minutes to go around the block. When he slowed in front of the gift shop again, there was no one waiting.

He was supposed to park as close as he could. He stopped. Five cars up ahead a brown sedan swung out from its place at the curb and went down the street. Either he was lucky or someone had been waiting to give him a place.

He drove ahead, backed quickly into the space, and turned off the engine. The afternoon sunlight cast purple shadows into the street and onto the far sidewalk, dimming his view of a man in a visor cap and a plaid wool shirt who was walking toward the drugstore.

He had saved the *Westphalia News* from the bus station, and now he pulled the folded copy out of his pocket and spread it on the steering wheel. For a few minutes he tried to read the news items. Then he turned the page, looked at a picture of a building under construction in Westphalia, read the caption, and gave up.

Hamilton was a one-way street, and cars came past him regularly, one after another, without hesitation. Most of the people on the sidewalk were headed toward Main and waited in groups at the crosswalk until the traffic stopped. A girl crossed the street. She had nice legs. A bus passed, sounding more like a train, its red lights blinked on and off and then glowed as it stopped at Main, blocking his view of the girl.

There was a movement on the sidewalk beside the car.

"I say, could I trouble you for the correct time?"

He was standing straight beside the car. Only the side of his coat was visible at the window.

It was five-fifteen by his wristwatch. "A little after five," he said.

"Do you know what time it is in Vienna?"

"I can give you Paris time."

"Splendid." The door swung open.

He came in sideways, hip first, his shoulders and head following. "Good evening, McAlister," he said.

He was short and heavy and stuffed in his overcoat like a sausage. He said, "I hope I did not keep you waiting too long. I'm a few minutes behind schedule."

"You're close enough."

There was a lot of flesh on his face, and he had a stubby nose and small round eyes. He was probably fifty-five or sixty, and there was nothing particularly unusual about him except that McAlister knew at once that he had seen him before.

He put his hat on his knees. "I presume everything has been satisfactory. You have the car. The clothes fit?"

"They fit."

"If you will put away that newspaper, we can start driving."

"Relax," McAlister said. "You just got here."

"I would rather talk with you as we drive."

"I like to know who I'm talking to."

"George," he said. "My name is George Knowles." He brought out a pack of cigarettes and held them out.

McAlister shook his head.

The Russian sat back and lit one carefully, puffed and blew the smoke out through pursed lips.

McAlister folded the newspaper and tucked it in the back of the seat. He said, "I've seen you before."

"Certainly. We saw each other in Moscow. You were in my office."

"You were at the post office this afternoon."

The Russian stared at him. His eyes were as bright as the eyes of a much younger man. "Yes," he said, "yes, of course. I was worried about you."

"You were pretty obvious. It would have been obvious to anyone else, too."

"No one else was watching."

"What were you doing at the post office?"

"I told you. I was worried about you."

"You didn't have to check on me."

"Not as it turned out, no. But I wanted to make sure that you got here."

"I got here," McAlister said.

"Alone," he said. "That you got here alone."

"You know better than that."

"There was always the possibility that you would come with someone else, perhaps the police."

"You know better than that, too."

"We should start. I want to show you the valley and the house where he lives, and it will be getting dark soon."

"Who did you think I'd be seeing at the post office?"

"I was looking for you, my boy."

"You weren't looking just for me. You didn't think I'd bring the police." McAlister looked at him. "You thought I'd be meeting someone else."

"That is possible. It could have happened."

"It didn't happen," McAlister said. "We are all co-operating. At least the Chinese are cooperating."

25

The Russian smiled for the first time. He had neat little teeth. "That is right," he said. "We may have our ideological differences, but when it comes to something like this, we work together. We must keep on cooperating."

"That was a hell of a way to cooperate."

"We should drive now." He puffed on the cigarette. "We can talk as we go."

"Relax for a minute," McAlister said. "I met a lot of people in Moscow. Where'd I meet you?"

"Perhaps you would recognize me in uniform." He put on the hat. "We talked for only a few minutes, but you were in my office for many hours."

Square on his head the hat gave him an air of pugnacious authority, and pinpointed his familiarity.

"The General," he said. "It was your office. Your people gave me the briefing."

"Splendid, my boy," the General said. He smiled again.

They weren't taking any chances. They had sent a major general with the reputation of an old fox to do an agent's job.

McAlister said, "They sent you here."

"I have lived here for many years. I went back to see you in Moscow." He tapped his cigarette out in the ash tray. "Now we should start. We are taking chances sitting here."

"You took your chances at the post office."

"I did not go in until I saw you."

McAlister turned on the engine. Cars had been going by him steadily. He waited for a break in the traffic and pulled out slowly.

In Moscow they had called the General "The Fat Fox." It was a nickname the partisans had given him during World War II when he worked behind German lines in the Ukraine. But he was a major general now with an office in Kaljayev Palace. It was a big office with a high ceiling and a carpet and two huge windows.

The General's desk was between the windows, and if you looked out either one you could see the church with its round domes glistening in the winter sun, like peeled onions one on top of the other. A spear at the top pointed skyward.

McAlister stopped for the light at Main Street. "All right, General," he said, "which way do we go?"

"South," the General said, "to the left. We go south past the university until we reach highway number fifty-five, and then we turn left, east, and it is only a few minutes."

McAlister waited for the light. He swung left into Main Street. Traffic was still heavy.

"You've been up here before?"

"A number of times," the General said. He looked at McAlister and smiled, showing his little teeth. "In preparation for your arrival. I have also gone by the woman's home in Colorado, just to make sure."

The traffic was picking up speed, and McAlister watched the car ahead. "All right," he said. "You wanted to talk. I'm listening."

The General lit a fresh cigarette and leaned back against the seat to enjoy his smoke. It was a few seconds before he spoke. "Your contact with Doctor Hermann is set for tomorrow."

"That's too soon."

"It's all set, my boy. You make the contact tomorrow, and you can take him right out there."

"I want to go out there first, before any contact."

"You have to meet them tomorrow."

"That's more important out there, and I want to check some things."

"You don't have to check anything."

The street was crossed with shadows and sunlight. Traveling just ahead of them was a station wagon. Children were playing in the back.

"Who scheduled it?"

"I did. Your friends, the Chinese, agreed."

"They don't have anybody here to agree."

"They have the one who recruited Hermann, Felix Klass. He wants the contact as soon as possible. We agreed on tomorrow."

"It's too soon."

"You must move quickly."

"Why?" he said. "What's the hurry?"

"We're all cooperating, McAlister, but we're cooperating to get the job done, not to delay. Every hour you delay, the more chance there is that something will go wrong."

"I don't trust him," McAlister said, "and I have to be sure of the girl."

"He's an old man," the General said. "His wife died more than five years ago. Your friends have spent more than a year checking all the facts. You saw the file. He worked for years as a consultant."

"For the military," McAlister said. "And maybe for the

Central Intelligence Agency." He watched the kids playing in the back of the station wagon ahead.

"There is no indication he has ever worked for Intelligence."

They drove in silence.

McAlister glanced at him, a fat little man with a bullet head, an ex-cop or an aging clerk who had eaten too well for too many years, his face thick and ruddy and stupid except for the bright little eyes. Knowles was setting himself up as the case officer, which is why he had been in Moscow and why they had used his office for the briefing. McAlister was supposed to be impressed.

They had briefed him on the Minuteman missile and Dr. Karl A. Hermann and the mission, and they had showed him diagrams and detailed aerial maps. He even knew what her house looked like from the air, a small rectangle less than a kilometer from the silo. The General had come in just twice during the briefing, at the beginning and on the second day, and they had all been very respectful. It had been carefully staged so he would accept the General now, over here.

But he had told them right from the beginning, there wasn't going to be any case officer. He would do it his own way, and he wasn't working for the Russians.

"There's the university," the General said. He pointed left.

McAlister saw the big brick buildings back among the trees, and the roads and the asphalt parking lots, and then they went past the entrance. The sign said, "State University, Westphalia."

"He doesn't live on the campus?"

"It's only a few minutes," the General said. "The turnoff is just ahead."

McAlister saw the intersection. He slowed.

The General rolled down his window and tossed out his cigarette. He left the window open. The air was cold, and it made a lot of noise as it rushed into the car.

The station wagon ahead with the children in the back pulled away, flashing in the sunlight. It went past the intersection and on down the highway.

McAlister turned left. Route fifty-five was asphalt, and it stretched straight between trees and across the gently rolling land. Far ahead, a ridge loomed high and green and clear.

The General resumed the conversation where they had left off. "We don't think it's possible," he said. "He could not be working for the C.I.A."

"That's one of the things I'm going to find out."

"It would be wiser to get on with the job."

"For you, maybe," McAlister said. "Not for me. I'm going to go back, General."

"You and I are here to do a job. That's more important."

"It's no good."

"Suppose I order you?"

McAlister glanced at him and then at the road. They would soon be going uphill toward the ridge. He let a car pass them.

"Don't bother, General," he said softly. "I was in this business long ago, and I've run agents myself. I'm not going to be run, General. No buildups, no bullshit, no handling, no letdowns.

"Let's keep it straight, General. I'm my own agent. I'm

not Peking's, and I'm not yours, and I've thought about this for a long, long while. I'm going to do the job, but I'm also going to go back, and I'm going to do it all my own way."

"I am not the only one here to help you, my boy. There are others."

"I don't want you and I don't want anyone else."

"We have had to watch Klass. We have had to make sure about Dr. Hermann and the girl. You will need more assistance than you know."

"I'm still going to do it my way, and it's going to take a few days."

"Why didn't you say these things in Moscow?"

"Because I didn't want to argue about it."

The General backed himself into the corner against the door. "I see," he said. "What about your Chinese friends, my boy? Do they know about this?"

"They figured it. But I'm the only former C.I.A. man available. I'm sure as hell the only one they can put to work. I'm the only man you can use, and the only one you can sacrifice if you want to, and still be sure it won't backfire. That's why Peking wanted me, and that's why you wanted me."

He glanced at the General. "Because even if I get picked up, Washington can't make any charges. They can't make any noise at all about an old C.I.A. man."

They were going up the ridge. The road curved to the left between the trees. McAlister could hear the engine working.

"Dr. Hermann provides an unprecedented opportunity. You must move quickly to ensure that opportunity."

31

"Go to hell," McAlister said. "You may figure I'm expendable, but I don't."

"It is not a question of expendability," the General said. "You have a great opportunity. You may change the course of history, of disarmament. I mean that quite seriously, my boy. An opportunity to bring peace for the future, for generations."

"It won't work, General. I know what I'm doing and I know why I'm doing it. And I don't need any glory song.

"Maybe we'll force disarmament, maybe not. I figured it was worth the risk long ago, but I'm going to do it my way, General. No case officer."

For a few seconds they drove in silence, and then the General lit another cigarette. They broke out of the trees and into the sunlight at the top of the ridge. McAlister could see across a wide valley, green fields, trees, houses, and a distant ridge.

The General pointed through the windshield. "Just ahead there on the right," he said. "You can park and I will show you the valley."

"How about his house?"

"We can stop for a minute," the General said.

They had widened the road so tourists could park and look out at the valley. McAlister slowed, swung into the area and stopped. The valley was spread out before them.

"There is nothing I can do about it," the General said. "The contact is tomorrow, and you will have to meet them."

He unbuttoned his overcoat. "I have the airline tickets for you. You leave on a nine o'clock airplane. It gets you into New York City a little after eleven."

"What time is the contact?"

"Twelve noon. It is set up for the main waiting room in Grand Central Station in New York City."

He took out a large wallet and flipped it open. "I have photographs of them both," he said. "Klass will be wearing a polka dot tie. That was his idea. You'll ask the time."

"Then what?"

"You have to set a time to pick up Dr. Hermann." The General handed him a ticket envelope.

McAlister turned it and opened it. The ticket was for Allegheny Airlines, Flight 873A, departure 9:05 a.m., Westphalia.

"These are your friends," the General said, and smiled as he handed him the photographs.

McAlister had seen pictures of Dr. Karl A. Hermann before. He was an old man, thin, with rimless glasses, white hair, and a long wrinkled neck.

But he had never seen the other one, the agent. The photograph showed his head and shoulders. He had a round, clean-shaven face, and thick black hair.

"I thought he was Chinese," McAlister said.

"Your friends won't tell us a thing about him," the General said. "That's how they are cooperating." He put his wallet away. "We think he's a White Russian," he said. "He was a boy in Manchuria. Then his name was Kurlov. Now he calls himself Klass, Felix Klass."

"He's the one who recruited Hermann?"

"He's the one."

In the photograph the eyes were small, and it was impossible to tell if Kurlov or Klass had a mongoloid eye flap. "He could be part Chinese," McAlister said.

"If he's Kurlov, his mother was Chinese. But we're not sure, and your friends won't tell us."

"That's why you were at the post office. You thought I was meeting him."

The General smiled. "We don't trust him," he said. "After you study them, you should destroy those photographs."

"I will," McAlister said. He tucked the pictures into the ticket envelope and put the envelope in his coat pocket. "That's not a very good place for a contact."

"I agree with you, my boy, but they picked it. Klass is running Dr. Hermann. He insisted on New York City and the station."

"You don't trust Klass and I don't trust Hermann."

"Dr. Hermann will do the job. He has the skills. At Autonetics Corporation, he helped design the control system. He has the command system on tape." He tossed his cigarette out the window. "You just take care of him out there."

The valley was a series of neat fields and scattered woods, small homes and barns, stone walls and fence lines marked by bushes and hedges. He could see a steeple poking up above the trees in a village. A main road ran right down the center of the valley floor. The windshield of a car flashed in the sun.

"It's a pretty valley," McAlister said.

"He's going to bring it down here."

"Why here?"

34

"It has to go through atmosphere to be armed, and that takes about two thousand kilometers."

"He chose the valley?"

"He wants to bring it down in a valley like this, where it will do less damage, and he has the coordinates."

"Where does he live?"

The General pointed. "Near the steeple. Just the other side of the village. I want to show you his house before it gets dark."

A car pulled into the parking area and stopped. A man and a woman were in the front seat. A door opened and a little brown dog jumped out and ran across the asphalt and into the grass.

McAlister looked up the valley toward the north. In one of the fields a wagon was spreading a white cloud of lime. The tractor turned wide, pulling the wagon in a half circle and leaving the white dust settling behind.

It would wipe out the valley.

The General was lighting another cigarette.

McAlister was tired, and he rubbed his face with the back of his hand. He watched the little brown dog come trotting back to the car. The door was still open, and the dog jumped inside. The car didn't move.

"How many people do you think live in the valley?"

The General blew out a thin stream of smoke. "I have not made a count. Perhaps three hundred, perhaps four."

"That's a lot of people. Men and women. Kids, too."

The sunlight was turning lemon yellow. In an hour it would be dusk, and lights would go on in the scattered homes.

The General puffed on his cigarette again. "Perhaps three hundred," he said. His voice was soft.

"There was a little place in the Ukraine. It is flat there, too, not like this. It was a small peasant village. When we got there, they were all dead, even some children who hadn't been able to escape. We counted two hundred and four dead. I know. I counted them. That was a long while ago, my boy, a long while ago, but the people who are killed are always innocent."

He took a drag on the cigarette, holding it between his thick thumb and forefinger. Then he sat up and squashed it in the ash tray.

"Let's look at his house and get back," he said. "We are both tired, and you've got a lot to do tomorrow."

McAlister started the car. The other car with the little dog had not moved. The man and woman were eating sandwiches, the door still wide open.

McAlister backed up a little and then drove forward. The dog had begun to bark. They headed downhill toward the floor of the valley.

Chapter 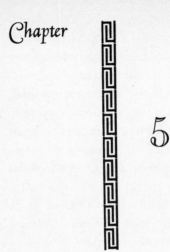 5

"SHALL we begin?" General Whooten said, chewing on an unlit cigar.

Except for Lieutenant James W. Ligett, all the men seated around the conference table were in civilian clothes.

"How about it, Harry?" the General said. "Let's get started."

"Yes, sir," Captain Harry Rivers said, standing up. He was tall. He had to lean over the table to open his manila folder and examine the page of notes he had prepared for the conference.

Lieutenant Ligett watched him. The Captain had met him downstairs and brought him up through the wide corridors of the Central Intelligence Agency.

"All right, gentlemen," General Whooten said. "If we can

37

have your attention, we'll get started. Lieutenant Ligett was kind enough to fly down from New York, and it's after five o'clock. We'd like to get out of here."

He looked at the far end of the table. "Colonel Rynders and Mr. Cummings, we'd like you to join us, too."

The two men were still talking. One of them wore thick glasses. "You go ahead, General," he said, smiling and cocking his head to one side. "We'd like to hear what the Lieutenant has to say." There was something wrong with his eyes. Even behind the thick glasses they didn't seem to focus right.

Captain Harry Rivers said, "Thank you, Colonel Rynders," and looked around the table. He straightened his page of notes.

"I have explained to Lieutenant Ligett that this is an official meeting of the Operating Intelligence Board. Our chairman, General Whooten, represents the Defense Intelligence Agency on the U.S.I.B., the Intelligence Board which correlates and coordinates intelligence estimates and functions."

He looked down at Lieutenant Ligett. "The O.I.B. is set up under the U.S.I.B. to deal with interservice studies and problems that don't fit properly within the purview of any particular agency."

"All right," the General said. "We can get into that crap some other time." He took the cigar out of his mouth. "Lieutenant, some of us heard what you said on tapes, but we're more interested in what you saw."

"Yes, sir," Ligett said. More than a dozen men were watching him. Captain Rivers had told him they represented

38

all the major intelligence agencies as well as the State Department.

"We were climbing," he said, "and I just happened to look at the Soviet's tail and something fell. I didn't have any idea what it was and I swung out and came around to get a look at it. At first I thought it was some part of the aircraft, but then I realized it was a man."

"Excuse me," Colonel Rynders said. "You had plenty of light?" He peered through his glasses.

"It was a full moon. I could see him against the clouds."

"What we are trying to establish, Lieutenant, is whether you saw a man, a parachutist, and *not* a dummy or some part of the aircraft or something else. It is rather important, because we have reason to believe they may have been trying to create an incident."

"Things were moving pretty fast," Lieutenant Ligett said. "I was pretty sure at the time, sir."

"That's why we asked you down here," Captain Harry Rivers said.

"How high were you, Lieutenant?"

"We'd been climbing steadily. About twenty-four, twenty-five thousand feet when he dropped."

Captain Rivers said, "Radar contact put it at twenty-five."

"That's high," the General said. "But it's not too high if they planned it that way." He looked down the table. "A professional could do it from that altitude, wouldn't you say, Gene, if they had worked it out carefully?"

Gene Cummings was a big man with a lean and handsome face. He was sitting next to Colonel Rynders with his arms folded across his chest. "Yes, of course, General," he

39

said. "It wouldn't be too difficult with an oxygen bottle."

Captain Rivers said, "The Air Force told me anything under twenty thousand and you don't have any real problems."

"They were supposed to be at thirty thousand," Colonel Rynders said.

"But they weren't," the General said. He pulled the cigar out of his mouth. "Your people just didn't want to believe our information."

"Two reliable sources," Captain Harry Rivers said, peering down the table. "Both of them out of East Germany. They said they'd bring him in, and one of them even said they might drop him."

"They confirmed each other," the General said. "You chose to ignore them."

"The Agency knew it was possible," Cummings said. He sat forward and unfolded his arms. "But they had to take a risk, a calculated risk." He tapped his right fist into his left palm. "It just didn't work out."

"You're damn right it didn't," the General said, putting the cigar back in his mouth.

"He's going to kill somebody," Captain Rivers said.

The room was silent. Lieutenant Ligett could hear the cool air coming out of the ducts. He watched the General as he struck a match, lighting his cigar.

"I still have my doubts," someone said. "It's just too far out." He was a swarthy man sitting on the other side of Colonel Rynders. "A Chinese agent," he said, "and the Russians drop him, and we aren't really sure why."

"We can guess," Captain Rivers said. "He's a KGB wet agent, an assassin."

"But there just isn't that kind of cooperation between the Russians and the Chinese. How the hell would your people in Frankfurt have detailed information on a Chinese agent being dropped by the Soviets? If they planned something like this, they'd keep it under tight security. Yet Defense Intelligence had two similar reports. It's too far out, Harry."

"We stand by our sources," the General said. He puffed on the cigar. "Furthermore, Mr. Maxwell, we've been working with the information. Harry thinks we may have a lead."

"Now wait a minute," Rynders said. He took off his thick glasses and rubbed the bridge of his nose. Everyone waited for him.

Watching and listening to them, Lieutenant Ligett realized that there were two competing groups here composed of the General and Captain Rivers from Defense Intelligence on one side, Colonel Rynders, Maxwell, and maybe Gene Cummings on the other.

"Lieutenant Ligett," Colonel Rynders said, "we're depending on what you saw, and it's rather important. Did Captain Rivers have a chance to explain the situation to you?"

"I didn't have time to give him any background."

Rynders put his glasses back on. "Well, Lieutenant," he said. "You're aware of the importance of the Menshikov mission. As you probably know, the Menshikov faction has been in control in the Kremlin for a few months. It is our best estimate that they really want to achieve disarmament. What's more important, we believe that the only way they're going to stay in power is to actually reach some kind of agreement."

Lieutenant Ligett nodded, wondering what the Colonel was getting at. For the first time, he noticed that Rynders had a scar over his left eye.

"There is another faction," the Colonel continued, "who claim a disarmament agreement is impossible—the old guard, the Army and the KGB. They're still pushing for heavy defense. We have reason to believe that they may be seeking to create an incident that would destroy the disarmament talks. So you can understand the importance of what you saw."

"You mean they were trying to create an incident?"

"That's one possibility," Rynders said. "The Army or the KGB could do it, and the Menshikov people might not know a thing about it."

"We don't buy that," Captain Rivers said.

For a few seconds the room was quiet.

"We know your position," Colonel Rynders said softly. "But the President doesn't agree with you, and he wants a disarmament agreement."

"How about it, Lieutenant," Captain Rivers said. "How sure are you that it was a man?"

"I was sure before I came down here," Lieutenant Ligett said, "but now I'm not so sure." He smiled and looked around the table. No one smiled back.

"At first," he said, "when I saw him, I thought it was gear, but I swung out and around." He put his hand up to the side. "Then I picked him up, and he was spreading out, his arms and his legs. I could see him against the clouds. It had to be a man."

"But you never saw a parachute?" It was the swarthy man, Maxwell.

"No, sir. I wanted to follow him down, but Major Conklin ordered me back. He didn't want me to follow him through the clouds."

"So he disappeared," someone said. "We don't even know that his parachute opened or that he got down."

"He got down all right," the General said. "He was a professional. The Lieutenant saw him straighten out, didn't you, Lieutenant?"

"I think so, sir."

"D.I.A. had surveillance responsibility," Maxwell said.

"Minimum surveillance," Captain Rivers said. "Minimum. We did everything that was possible or feasible. We counted them on that airplane at Ottawa and we counted them off in Washington. Counter Intelligence checked their aircraft. Some of their people were coming here commercial, and we've had customs and immigration alerted for a week now. But we couldn't do a thing about the drop, Maxwell, because of your specific instructions. Minimum surveillance and no actions that could cause an incident."

Maxwell said, "It was a crazy way to deliver an agent."

"It wasn't so crazy," the General said. "They succeeded. They got him in clean, right past us. The Lieutenant here couldn't even follow him down."

"Suppose he had," Maxwell said. "What good would that have done?"

"He could have given us a location," the General said. "The Bureau or the C.I.C. could have picked him up."

"He'd be talking," Captain Rivers said. "We'd have him squeezed dry by now, or dead." He looked at the man sitting across the table from Lieutenant Ligett. "Isn't that true, Charlie?"

The man was fleshy in the jowls. A late shave had left his cheeks smooth and shiny. He took his cigarette from his lips.

"We probably could have picked him up," he said. "It would depend on just where he came down. There's a lot of mountains up there. But it would have made the job a lot easier, I'll say that. Now he's got a twelve-hour start on us, and all we can do is routine checking and hope for a break."

The General said, "The Bureau's working on it?"

"They've been on it since last night," Maxwell replied.

"I thought it was Defense Intelligence responsibility?" asked Harry Rivers.

"Your people are involved," Maxwell said.

"Then C.I.A. is taking over," the General said. "Is that right, Colonel Rynders, your people are taking responsibility?"

"We have to work together," Colonel Rynders said. "I asked Maxwell to get it organized because the Director wants the Agency on top of it. But it's your show, too, General."

"All right," the General said. "If it's a joint operation, we'd like to have Gene running it. He was with Defense Intelligence long enough to know our kind of operation."

Rynders took off his glasses and rubbed his eyes again,

and there was silence for a moment. "We have to work together," he said, "across the board, and I'm sure Maxwell
won't mind giving it up."

"Not a bit," Maxwell said, staring at the General.

"If Gene wants to do it, maybe that's a good idea," Colonel Rynders added.

"I think we can move pretty fast," Gene Cummings said.

"We worked out a few leads," the General said. "Just in
case our information was correct. I was telling Gene about it
before the meeting." He dropped the cigar butt into the ash
tray.

He looked up at Captain Rivers. "You have a cigar,
Harry? I'm all out."

The Captain dug a cigar from the pocket inside his suit
jacket and offered it to the General. He took it, bit the end
and spat it delicately aside. Captain Rivers snapped open his
lighter. The flame jumped. The General puffed once, twice,
and blew out a thick stream of smoke.

He said, "We took the position that our information is ac-
curate, right down the line, and that he's here on a mission,
maybe a wet job. If that's so, they have to have a reason for
not sending him with the ambassador or on false papers.
Dropping him isn't an easy way to deliver him."

He took out his cigar and looked at it. "Captain Rivers
figured maybe the agent is known. Maybe he's been in the
States before. Maybe they were afraid he would be recognized. He could be someone we kicked out.

"He's a Chinese agent. And that makes sense if he was
one of the Chinese students that went back or one of the sci-
entists. There were a lot of them.

45

"I won't go into all the work that Captain Rivers and his people did. Among other things, they ran all the information through WALNUT, looking for correlations. The computers came up with a couple of possibilities. One of them is pretty good." He puffed on his cigar.

"We think it's a good possibility," Captain Rivers said.

"Colonel Rynders," the General took over, "the Agency did a lot of drop and pickup work during the Korean War, didn't it?"

"That was a long time ago, almost twenty years ago," Colonel Rynders said.

"One of your planes went down in China. They shot the Chinese you had aboard and threw your people into prison." The General puffed on his cigar. "What happened to those men?"

"The pilot died. They let the Air Force man out."

"The other ones?" Captain Harry Rivers said. "What happened to the C.I.A. men?"

"There were only two of them."

"Where are they now?" the General questioned.

"They're serving life sentences."

"But they're out of prison," Captain Rivers said. "They have been out of prison for some time."

The General waved his cigar gently back and forth over the table. "I'm suggesting we should look into it, gentlemen. They've been over there a long while."

"It's a possibility, of course," Maxwell said. "We'll check it out. But they're still Agency men, General. They wouldn't work for the Chinese or anyone else."

"A lot happens to a man in twenty years, Mr. Maxwell."

Captain Harry Rivers said, "Gene knew both of them, and he worked with them out there. He may be able to move pretty fast. That's one of the reasons we'd like to have him running the show."

Gene Cummings was leaning forward. He had unfolded his arms, and now he tapped his right fist into his open left palm. "I told the General it was a possibility," he said.

"I knew them both pretty well." He looked down at his hands and then around the table. "My wife was married to one of them," he said. "We all knew each other when we were young."

The room was silent.

Colonel Rynders said, "You sure you want to run it?"

"It's all right," Cummings said. "If it is one of them, I should be able to get him faster than anyone else."

"I don't think it is," Colonel Rynders retorted.

"Maybe we'll have some luck," the man from the Bureau said.

"We'd better," Captain Harry Rivers said. "The President's going to be meeting with those people."

No one spoke.

General Whooten puffed on his cigar. Then he said, "All right, gentlemen. We've got a couple of minor items to cover. But we might as well let Lieutenant Ligett go first. With our thanks, Lieutenant."

Ligett pushed back his chair and got up to stand beside Captain Rivers.

"One other thing, Lieutenant," the General said. "You'll have to consider everything that went on here top secret. You're to discuss it with no one, neither your commanding officer nor your wife. You can consider that a formal order."

"Yes, sir."

"We appreciate your coming down," the General said. "Captain Rivers will show you out."

Rivers went ahead of him to open the door. At the end of the table, Colonel Rynders stood up and stuck out his hand. "Thanks for coming down," he said, peering. "It was a great help to all of us."

Ligett shook his hand. "It was my pleasure, sir."

Captain Rivers was waiting for him. He went through the doorway and Rivers pulled it shut after them.

They started down the wide, windowless corridor. There was no way to tell whether it was daylight or night outside. He thought it was probably after six o'clock by now.

"Who's Colonel Rynders?" Ligett asked.

"He's deputy director at the Agency."

"He's got something wrong with his eyes."

Most of the offices were dark and empty, their doors shut. They went by one where the lights were on. Their footsteps echoed.

"The story is that he was hurt in the war," Rivers said. "World War II."

"Who was?" Lieutenant Ligett said, turning the corner near the elevators. He had been thinking that if he was lucky he would get back in time to stop in at the Turners' party.

"Colonel Rynders," Rivers said.

"He seemed like a nice guy," Ligett said. He smiled. "A lot of brass in that room."

"You handled it nicely," Captain Rivers said. "I'll make

48

sure you get a formal letter of thanks over the General's sig-nature."

The elevator doors opened. They stepped aboard. Captain Rivers said, "There's a car waiting to take you back to the base."

When the elevator stopped, they walked down a short corridor, past an empty desk, and then past a young man in a suit coat. He nodded to the Captain. They emerged from the building into the late sunlight.

A low building jutted out to their left like an arm, en-closing the wide court which was mostly cement with a square of grass in the center. Beyond the court, there were trees everywhere. The C.I.A. headquarters had been planted in the middle of the woods. A sedan was parked to the right at the edge of the steps.

"That's him," Captain Rivers said. "He'll take you out."

The car glistened deep blue in the soft light. It had Vir-ginia license plates.

Captain Rivers pulled the back door open and stuck out his hand. "Thanks again," he said.

"Happy to do it," Ligett said, shaking the hand. He got in. The door slammed, and the car started almost at once. It swung around the square of grass and headed away from the building.

Lieutenant Ligett looked out the back window. It was a huge cement building, white in the dusk, seven or eight sto-ries high. The only glass was on the ground floor, and above the glass the wide front was faced with rows of short cement columns, like fluting. Off to the side near the entrance was a dome, curving above the trees like a mausoleum.

A guard waved them on.

Lieutenant Ligett leaned forward. "How long will it take us to get to the base?"

The driver was a young man with long hair. "From Langley here, it should take about twenty minutes unless we get caught in traffic."

"Thanks," Ligett said. The car stopped. They were going to turn onto the highway.

He looked out the rear window again. A sign at the roadside read, "Bureau of Public Roads." Through the trees he could make out parts of the huge building.

Lieutenant Ligett sat back and rubbed his chin. He needed a shave, and he was wondering if he should take the time to telephone Lucy from the base and tell her he would be home by midnight, and that he would meet her at the Turners' party.

6

McALISTER was late for the contact. His airplane was behind schedule landing at LaGuardia Airport, and he had spent a few minutes putting his things in a locker before finding a taxi to take him into the city.

Everybody was hurrying. He walked through the wide tunnel into Grand Central Station, annoyed at himself for being nervous. He was going to have to make a lot of contacts. It was the worst part of the business, because only one of them had to go wrong, and it would all be over.

There was a bookstall in the middle of the corridor, and beyond that the wide station and the round information booth around which people were standing, a girl in a tan coat and two men arguing.

He had been telling himself to relax all morning, trying

to nap on the airplane and then looking out the window on the way in from the airport. He had watched an airplane threading through the sky, the flashing cars speeding closely beside him, and the greenish water of the bay still as a lake. He had seen the city from the bridge, towers poking up high through the haze and sunlight, a world apart from anything he had known for many years.

It was just eighteen minutes after twelve by the clock. The waiting room was to the south. He had to go through another short corridor. He walked past people, some of them rushing away, some standing. The corridor sloped upward, lined with many doors. He went through one of them.

Straight ahead was a brightly lit newspaper stand. To the right and left were double rows of heavy benches filled with people. Most of them were men, some reading open newspapers in the dingy light, others staring blankly at the floor or at the walls. One old man was sleeping with his head back and his mouth open.

McAlister turned right and walked down along the outside of the benches. They shouldn't have picked a waiting room. Everyone is waiting and watching, and you don't have any options. You have to take the chance.

Then he saw them sitting beside each other, one tall and the other short. The old man had an open book on his knees. He was looking straight ahead with his glasses high on his nose and his head jutting forward on his long neck. He looked about seventy years old, a harmless old man with a slightly senile smile across his face.

The other one, Klass, was short and fat. His face was

round as a moon, and he was wearing a polka dot tie. A newspaper was spread open on his lap.

McAlister glanced around the room. But you couldn't tell anything by looking at the people. He walked back to the newsstand and bought an afternoon paper. He scanned the front page, and then went back to the end of the bench. No one was paying any attention to him.

There was a space on the far side of Klass. He stepped between the benches, worked his way past them, and sat down. Carefully, he opened the newspaper, folded it down the center and read the headlines.

"Disarm Talks Open." He read the story carefully, taking his time.

"The Soviet Disarmament Mission headed by Premier A. S. Menshikov began talks today with top-level technical experts of both the State Department and the Arms Control and Disarmament Agency.

"Still key to the technical talks, according to State Department sources, is the question of inspection that would encompass launch control and satellite command centers. Without such inspection, there is no way to measure or equalize systems already in place, which some experts claim may change the balance of power and force a new round of even more sophisticated missile-control satellites.

"Both powers have now indicated a willingness to limit installation of the satellite-controlled defense systems, which can limit but not prevent offensive missile penetration. However, most experts concede, mutual inspection of all launch and control centers is the only feasible basis for a workable agreement.

"Observers in Washington today were the most optimistic they have been in years about the hopes . . ."

McAlister continued to hold the newspaper as if he were reading it. "Excuse me," he said, turning to Klass, "my watch is running a little fast. Do you have the correct time?"

Klass peered at him. There was no surprise and no interest on his moon face, but his eyes kept blinking slowly.

"Why certainly," he said. He pulled a fob from below his belt, got out his watch and looked at it. There was nothing Chinese about him. If he were Kurlov or Klass, he had inherited neither skin color nor eyes from his mother.

"It's just twelve-thirty," he said. "Is that what you wanted?"

"What would that be Paris time?"

"I can give you London time," he said quickly. He tucked his watch back into his pocket. He said, "We were worried you weren't coming. Are you alone?"

"Yes," McAlister said. "Why?"

"He is not with you?" He blinked again. He was very nervous, too.

"I told you I'm alone."

"I think we saw him. Mr. Knowles. He was in here before."

"Who was?" The General had no business here. It was bad enough with the two of them.

"He is their man here. He has contacted me."

"What's he doing here?"

"We would like to know that, too." He sat up a little, looking over the benches toward the newsstand.

McAlister lowered his newspaper and followed his glance.

54

But there was nothing unusual. A woman with white hair was buying a magazine.

Klass said, "You are taking orders from them?"

"I'm taking orders from nobody."

"He is not here to give orders. He is here to help."

"All right," McAlister said. "He has helped."

"You will take Dr. Hermann out there alone, without him?" He blinked, but there was still no expression on his face.

"I'll take him out there," McAlister said. He didn't come here to talk about the General. "He'll have to do the job alone."

"It must be done while the mission is still in Washington."

"I know that."

"And I will give him final instructions," Klass said.

"All right," McAlister said. "You can give him any orders you want. I'd like to talk to him."

"Yes," Klass said, "yes, of course." He peered at McAlister with his black eyes, and then he blinked again. He said softly in Chinese, "How was your wife?"

McAlister hardly heard the words, and he wasn't thinking in Chinese. He said, "What?"

"How was your wife?"

Klass had picked a place like this for a contact but he was being very careful.

McAlister answered him in Chinese. "Her name is Tu-chan," he said. "Speak in English."

Klass turned to speak to Dr. Hermann. "This is the man," he said. "His name is Hamill, Albert Hamill."

55

Dr. Hermann bent forward, stretching out his long neck to look around Klass. "We have been waiting for you, Mr. Hamill," he said. "When do we start?"

"I will get up so you can talk," Klass said. He seemed heavier standing, a short man in a double-breasted black silk suit. His shoes were polished to a blue-black luster.

McAlister lifted his newspaper again and looked at the old man. The eyes were large behind the rimless glasses, and he was smiling.

McAlister said, "Where can I reach you?"

"At the State University." His voice was scratchy. There was a trace of an accent. "It is near Westphalia, and I am in the telephone book."

"Are you sure you can do it?"

"Oh, yes, oh yes." His head bobbed up and down. "It has been my work for many years. I can do what is necessary." He smiled again, still nodding, trying to be friendly. "You may be confident."

"How much equipment?"

"Two suitcases. They will be ready." He leaned forward. "It will only take a little while," he said. "A little while. But I must depend on you to get me there."

"I'll get you there and out, too."

"When, Mr. Hamill?"

"I have some things to do. Let's figure three or four days, the weekend. I'll telephone you by the weekend."

"If you telephone through the university switchboard, you will need to be careful of what you say."

"I will be careful," McAlister said, smiling. It didn't make any sense, but he liked the old man.

56

Klass sat down suddenly, putting his bulk between them. He had his overcoat over his arm. "I think that is enough," he said. "If we need to talk further, we can go somewhere else."

They were silent for a moment. McAlister lowered the newspaper and glanced around the room. A middle-aged man in a pressed suit with a vest was peering at them as he went by. He was walking slowly, looking for a place to sit.

"Your friend has been here," Klass said, "and it is time we left. You and Dr. Hermann can identify each other. You can work together."

McAlister said, "You're not going to be with us?"

"No," he said, blinking. "But I will give Dr. Hermann final instructions." His face was still without expression.

"Where can I find you?"

Klass stared at him. "You do not need to find me," he said.

"Does Dr. Hermann know where to reach you?"

Klass sat silently for a second. "It would not be smart to look for me," he said. "But if you must reach me, you can see a man you once knew, Sidney Borland. Do you remember him?"

"How do you know Borland?"

Klass smiled faintly. "We have spent a long while preparing for this, Mr. Hamill, and we have investigated everything. He was helpful about your past, although he did not realize what it was all about."

"Borland?"

"I should caution you. He is not with us. He doesn't understand, and it will be dangerous to talk to him. But if you must try to find me, he may be of help."

"Isn't there any drop, any contact?"

"There is no need," Klass said. "But someday we may see each other again." He gave a little smile.

Dr. Hermann got up holding his book in one hand and buttoning his brown tweed overcoat with the other. He smiled again, nodded and said, "I will be waiting for you."

He stepped past them, skinny and tall, and went around the edge of the bench, walking with his head bent forward.

McAlister lifted his newspaper again. Apparently they were clean, because anybody who had been waiting for the contact would have moved by now. There wasn't any point in being nervous.

"Dr. Hermann is going through the station," Klass said. "I'll go out onto the street here. Give me a few minutes."

He got up holding his overcoat over his arm and stepped past McAlister and around the edge of the bench. McAlister watched his broad back. Klass paused at the newsstand, looked around, and then turned right, heading toward the street.

Neither Klass nor the old man was the kind of man you would choose for a thing like this. But it wasn't a matter of choice, and it didn't really make any difference now. When it was over the old man and Klass would disappear, and he would disappear, too, which was all he really wanted. He would be with Tu-chan while the boys grew up.

He glanced at his watch. It was exactly twelve-fifty. His return ticket was for a five o'clock airplane. He had a few hours. He would wait twenty minutes to give Dr. Hermann and Klass plenty of time.

They had checked on him here, in the States, back to Borland. He should have known they would do that. Borland was the only one who got out after the crash. He was supposed to get them all out, but he had disappeared. That was twenty years ago and still they had found Borland and talked to him.

He would walk for a while. He would walk crosstown, and perhaps down to Macy's. He could remember shopping there when he was a kid. His mother had taken him there whenever they came into the city.

At one-ten he got up and passed around the benches and the newsstand and went out into the street.

The sidewalks were crowded with people, and traffic jammed the street. There was a big bus with advertising on its side right in front of him. Far away a siren was howling.

He turned right and joined the moving crowds. Just ahead at the edge of the sidewalk there was a knot of people. As he got closer, he saw that they were gathered around a policeman standing in front of a patrol car. A horn honked. Traffic was trying to pass. The red light on top of the car was flashing.

The big policeman waved his billy at the passers-by. "Keep moving along, please," he said, "move along."

Somebody bumped McAlister. He jumped aside, but it was just a boy pushing in close to see. McAlister let him go past and then followed him into the edge of the shifting bodies.

The siren came from far down the street.

"Move along please," the big cop repeated. "Don't block the sidewalk. Move along please."

Behind him, another cop was crouching on the sidewalk. McAlister looked between the people.

The cop was holding an oxygen cylinder and a little white mask against the face of a heavy man who lay half on his side and half on his back on the edge of the sidewalk. His black silk suit shone in the sunlight. His blue polka dot tie was pulled aside as if he had torn his collar trying to get his breath.

It was Felix Klass, and he was dead.

The cop stood up, holding the oxygen cylinder with the mask swinging at the end of the tube.

The siren was coming closer. It was an ambulance.

The big cop was still waving his billy. "Move along, please."

Someone asked, "What happened?"

"Fellow had a heart attack," a man said.

"Move along, please," the cop said.

McAlister moved closer through the crowd.

With its siren screaming, the ambulance swung in behind the police car. A young man in an open white coat came out of the cab, walking rapidly, and the siren wailed off.

The crowd pressed in. The big cop stood at Klass's feet, beside the polished shoes.

"Coronary?" the young man asked.

"I tried oxygen, but I didn't get any pulse."

The attendant kneeled and pulled at the man's eyelids.

The cop said, "You want the resuscitator?"

The attendant shook his head.

"Move along, please. Now just keep moving."

"Coronary," the attendant said and stood up. "Let's get him out of here." He looked back at the ambulance. Another man was coming with a stretcher.

"Come on," the big cop said, "let's keep it moving. Don't block the sidewalk."

James McAlister turned away from the curb and pushed through the crowd. His right knee was twitching.

An autopsy would list the cause of death as a heart attack or heart failure. But it was not a coronary. Potassium cyanide leaves no trace. From right up close someone had fired potassium cyanide into Felix Klass's moon face. They had taken a chance, here in the sunlight on the sidewalk in the middle of the city.

They made spray guns in compact forms, an umbrella or a pack of cigarettes or a cigar you could hold in your mouth. After you fired, you sniffed an antidote. But you were taking a chance to use it when there were other people around.

Whoever did it would have been a few steps past him when Klass collapsed. Klass had died within seconds from constriction of the blood vessels.

McAlister looked back. The crowd was watching as they started to move the body. It could have been the Russian, or it could have been the C.I.A., or anyone else. But it wouldn't make sense if it was the Russian. Someone else had been there. Someone knew of the contact. The thing to do was to walk, to run.

He walked fast, his hands in his coat pockets, squeezing his thumbs with his fingers in time with his steps, watching the faces and the people as he threaded his way. With this many people, he couldn't check if he was being followed, but he could lose them. He was getting warm from walking fast in the sunshine, but his knee had stopped twitching.

He would have to disappear for a day or so. But there was no place to go. Except out there, to Colorado. He had to go out there soon, anyway. And nobody knew about it except the General and maybe some of Klass's people, but they wouldn't expect him to go there now, alone, without Hermann. He would be safe for a few days, and it wouldn't waste any time because, from the beginning, he had planned to visit her and set it up.

He stopped at a street corner and waited for the light to change. A taxicab stopped in front of the curb. A girl got out sideways, hoisting her handbag strap over her shoulder.

McAlister stepped through the crowd. "Taxi," he said, and reached out behind the girl to catch the door. He ducked inside, sat down, and pulled the door closed.

"North," he said, "go north for a few blocks."

"Yes, sir," the driver said, shoving down the flag. The cab started.

McAlister turned around quickly. No one else was trying to hail a cab.

"Where to, sir?"

"North," he said.

"But where do you want to go north?"

"Oh," McAlister said. "Macy's."

"That's south, sir, downtown."

"All right," McAlister said.

"You sure now that's where you want to go?"

"Yes," McAlister said. "I'm sure, thanks."

"Any special corner at Macy's?"

"Any corner is all right."

The cab was warm. He sat back in the seat and closed his eyes, listening to the traffic outside.

Chapter

7

McALISTER had slept most of the way on the airplane, and he had gained a few hours flying west. Using his Avis charge, he rented a car at the airport and drove north from Denver.

It was dark by the time he reached the intersection a few miles before the city of Greeley, and turned east. The road was asphalt, two cars wide. He drove for miles through the darkness while the land rolled gently off to each side. Now and then his lights made the low places look like water, like the land near the river where at night you can see the paddies black and shiny.

A traffic light blinked orange. He slowed and made the turn, heading north, passing a few clumps of trees and dark fields. The low ridge was just ahead.

The sign, "Air Force Installation, Winesap II," marked his next turn right. The asphalt became hard dirt and the road climbed slowly. Soon he was high enough to look across the shallow valley at the scattered lights to the north. It was less than a mile to her house.

It was an old farmhouse, small and white with green shutters, just as she had described it. He touched the brakes and slowed. The porch light was on. On the step by the door was a bright red bowl, a dog's bowl. And he could see the big tree and the swing at the side of the house. She had written him about the swing, telling him that she had put it up for some kids down the road, but they never used it.

He pulled off onto the grass shoulder, snapped off the headlights and sat for a minute in the sudden darkness and quiet.

From here, for years, she had written him every few weeks, putting her letters in the mailbox by the side of the road, only a hundred meters in front of him. Her letters had come through Hong Kong, arriving in rumpled envelopes, her neat printing often smeared.

At first she had written of Hallee, who had been in pain, but so full of opium that he had smiled and smiled, not knowing that he was dying. Then for a long while, after she married again, there were no letters. The marriage hadn't worked and when she moved out here, some five years ago, she started writing again—about her house and the little school where she was teaching, her classroom and the children, about the things she did, the people she knew, and about her dog. In the spring she wrote about Hallee, because it had been spring when they had gone down and when he had died, and she still could not forget.

If anyone had been censoring her mail they had missed or permitted—perhaps wanted—her to tell of the missile silo she had watched being dug in the lowland less than a kilometer from her house. Those few stray paragraphs in her letters had been read somewhere, and sent on to Bow Street Alley. Those paragraphs had brought him here, as well as the General, and maybe they had killed Felix Klass.

His thoughts turned to the countryside. It had been every shade of gray in the photographs, and he knew where the main road was, and the houses. Looking south, he could see the cluster of lights that would be the Air Force installation, a barracks and headquarters. Buried underground, some fifty feet, was the launch control center.

He got a handkerchief out of his back pocket and wiped his face. He put on his tie, and then his suitcoat. It was important to look respectable: coming at night like this, he did not want to frighten her.

He swung into the driveway and stopped behind a green Ford. A dog had started barking, and then trotted out from the other side of the car as he got out.

"It's all right, fellow," McAlister said. He took his overcoat from the seat and put it on, feeling the weight of the gun hanging in the pocket.

But the dog kept on barking. He walked to the front door and rang the bell. The door swung open.

She looked like her photographs. Her hair was brown, and she was wearing a light blue blouse and a skirt.

"Ann Learson?" he asked.

"Yes."

"My name's McAlister," he said. "James McAlister."

"Yes," she said again, but she didn't understand.

She stared at him out of eyes edged with lines.

"James McAlister?" she repeated, trying to place him.

He didn't want to frighten her. He smiled. "From China. We've been writing to each other for a long while."

"Oh, my God," she said and touched her fingers to her lips. "How did you get here?"

"It's all right," he said. "I drove up from Denver."

"I mean the United States. When did you come back to the States?"

"A few days ago."

"I got a letter from you, on Monday. You didn't say anything about coming."

"I couldn't write about it," he said. "I didn't have any choice."

"It's such a surprise."

"I'm sorry."

"No," she said. "No, it's all right. Won't you come in?"

She stepped back, opening the door wider. In the light he saw that she was a good looking woman with high cheekbones, a delicate mouth and a firm chin. He stepped into the little foyer. A staircase went up to the right. Straight ahead down the short hallway was the living room. He could smell the smoke of an open fire.

The front door closed behind him. He slipped out of his coat and hung it in the closet with the gun still in the pocket. It was taking a chance, but she knew he lived alone.

"James McAlister," she said, "after all these years. It's difficult to believe."

"It's difficult for me, too," he said.

She looked down at her hands. "What about your family? You wrote about them so much I feel I know them."

"I'm here alone."

"Are they coming later?"

"No," he said. He had to be careful what he told her. "But they're fine."

"It's just a visit, then?" she said.

"Perhaps a few days."

They walked into the living room. The remains of a few logs were still burning in the fireplace. She reached over and took a cigarette from a box on the coffee table.

McAlister had noticed the photographs on the mantel behind her, and went toward them, knowing for certain that one of them would be a picture of Captain Harold Lee, United States Air Force.

Framed in silver, he was wearing a sloppy Air Force hat. The face was thin, the eyes set deep and the skin dark, which was why they had always called him "the Indian." It was hard to realize it had been so many years ago.

McAlister said, "That's the first picture I've seen of him. He looks so damn young."

"He was twenty-five."

"That's right." He turned a little and walked to the big window. It faced west toward the mountains. He could see lights a little below them.

Hallee was buried in an out-of-the-way grave in northern

China where it got muddy every time it rained, and it rained often.

"Everyone's forgotten about it," she said. "Except me and your mother."

"I haven't forgotten," he said. "How is Mother?"

"She's fine. I spoke to her two weeks ago. She didn't say anything about your coming back."

"She doesn't know about it."

"You know, she still talks about your returning to the States to live. Are you going to see her?"

"I hope I can," he said. "I'm not going to be here very long, a few days at the most."

"Why does it have to be so short?"

She was standing by the side of the fireplace, straight and poised, and yet a little frightened. McAlister realized he knew as much about her, and as little, as he knew about anyone in the States.

"I'm afraid I'm in pretty deep, Ann. I believe I can trust you, and I need your help."

"Of course you can trust me."

"I came back because I thought I could get some answers. I want to find out about some things."

"What?"

"Who put our plane down in China."

"That was a long time ago."

"I promised Hallee I would find out someday."

"But it has been twenty years." McAlister detected a tremor in her voice.

"You never got over him, did you?"

"I suppose you're right," she said as she dropped her cigarette into the fireplace. "But I just don't think about it anymore. Sometimes I wake up at night, and I don't know why; I guess it has to be him."

"The Indian."

She smiled. "Nobody has called him that since I can remember." She turned away, visibly shaken.

"Care for another cigarette?"

"I'm okay," she said, "you just caught me unawares." She walked to the end of the couch. "I'd like to freshen up a little. I'll be right back."

"Can I get anything? Wood for the fire? Drinks?"

"The liquor's in the cabinet by the refrigerator. You could fix me a scotch and soda."

"All right," he said.

He watched her go, half running up the stairs, and then her steps sounded above him.

McAlister went to the picture window and once again stared out at the scattered lights in the dark valley.

It would be after midnight in Moscow and another day in China. If it were early morning, Tu-chan would be talking with the boys while the old lady, Tu-chan's aunt, worked at the stove, rattling the pans. Tu-chan had not believed his lie, that he had to spend two months studying new techniques of polymerization, that the plant was going to produce some new plastics. At night he had found her crying; the only thing she had wanted to know was that he would be coming back.

He had kissed her and looked at her for a long while, without speaking. Her black eyes had been wet with tears,

70

her skin golden in the moonlight. Then he had promised her, with all the sincerity of his own hopes, that it would be all right and that he would come back.

Weeks later, on the morning the truck came, she had asked for perhaps the sixth or seventh time if he would be back by summer, and he had repeated the lie that they were going to make him a better chemical engineer and that he did not know how long it would take. He had promised to write, and he had written every day, and then enough letters to cover all the time he might be gone. They were mailing one letter each day from Moscow.

He heard Ann coming down the stairs. He turned.

She came into the living room, stopped, and looked at him and then at the coffee table. "I thought you were going to fix drinks?"

"I forgot," he said. "I've been thinking, and trying to see out your window."

"That's not much of a view at night," she said. "In the daylight, you can see the mountains."

She had brushed her hair so that it glistened, and she had changed into a print blouse and a wool skirt that made her hips flat. "You look very nice," he said.

"Thank you," she said. She opened the front door to let in the dog, who had been whining outside. Rufus quickly made friends with McAlister and went to his favorite spot in the living room to lie down.

McAlister followed Ann into the kitchen. It was spotless except for a single used coffee cup left on the white table.

She opened the freezer and banged out an ice tray. "When

71

we were married," she said, "Hallee and I often talked about a house in the country. He liked the idea of living in the country."

"He would have liked it here."

She put a few cubes in each glass. "You always called him the Indian, didn't you? I never could understand why." She pointed to the cabinet. "The liquor's in there. You can get the scotch for me."

McAlister got out a bottle of bourbon and a bottle of scotch and put them on the counter. "He looked like an Indian," he said, "and he always claimed he was part Cherokee."

"He was no more Indian than I am." She laughed and put the glasses on the counter. McAlister fixed the drinks.

"You don't mind talking about him?" he asked after they had returned to the living room. Ann was sitting in one corner of the couch, her long legs folded under her. Rufus was asleep on the floor.

"No," she said. "I never believed the explanations they gave me."

"Borland was supposed to tell you the truth."

"The one who came back, the copilot. I didn't like him. He told me about the Central Intelligence Agency, but I already knew you had been working for them."

"Hallee and Borland had both volunteered, because we needed an Air Force crew with the airplane."

"I hope it was worth it."

He sat down on the coffee table. He had written her some of the facts but he had been in prison then, and he had had to phrase them very carefully.

72

"It was important at the time," he said. "We needed information on their troop and supply movements. It was a dangerous way to operate, but we had plenty of agents. They were Nationalist Chinese. We needed information fast, and the Agency had a new technique. At least it was new then."

"You mean that pickup business. Everyone denied it, but Borland did tell me that was true."

"The Chinese showed some of the equipment during the trial. Do you remember the pictures?"

"They had some wreckage of the plane, too."

"A harness and a nylon line," McAlister said. "Hallee would come in very low, and we had a pickup hook that grabbed the line. Nylon has a lot of stretch. We would pick the agent right off the ground. We never had to land, and we never lost a man on pickup."

She said, "You wrote those last letters for him, didn't you?"

"Yes," McAlister said. "They let me sit with him in the room. He dictated them."

"Was he in pain?"

"I don't think so, except for the coughing. Then he used to double up. They didn't give him any antibiotics. They didn't have any. If he'd had penicillin, he might have made it."

He picked up his glass. "During the last few days you could hear him breathing. They gave him opium, and I don't think he was in pain."

He said, "I'll get us another drink."

"That was pretty fast."

"I need it," he said.

"So do I," she said. She finished her drink and handed him the glass. He went into the kitchen and fixed refills, thinking about Hallee.

He hadn't thought about the details for a long while, but telling her brought it back.

The Indian had slept on his back, his breath rasping in and out. Sometimes he would wake up, his dark eyes blinking open.

"Hello, Indian," McAlister would say. "How are you making it?"

"Okay." He would lick his dark dry lips. "I've been thinking. It had to be one of our people."

"Don't you ever stop thinking about it?"

"You're going to do it for me, Jim."

"You'll do it for yourself. You'll find him. We'll do it together."

"I'll kill the son of a bitch if I make it."

"You'll make it. Your new lady doctor said you should start trying. She says you've been taking it pretty easy."

They kept the windows closed, so it was always hot in the room. It smelled of sweat.

"I can't even get out of bed to pee."

He would lick his lips again. After a few minutes, he would say, "Find out, Jim. Get the son of a bitch."

McAlister carried the drinks into the living room. She was standing behind the couch. She said, "It's getting cool. We can put some logs on the fire if you like."

"In a few minutes," he said. He gave her the drink. "What did Borland tell you? What do you remember?"

"I wasn't in very good shape in those days."

74

"Did he tell you it was sabotage? We weren't shot down. Someone put explosives aboard the plane."

"Everyone said you were shot down."

"They knew better." He drank a slug of the bourbon. "The Agency knew the truth, and they should have done something about it."

"Did Hallee know?"

"Someone put dynamite aboard the plane with a timer. Borland was supposed to raise hell and get us out. He was supposed to go to the newspapers if he had to. The Agency could have gotten us out. They could have made an exchange, if nothing else."

"Maybe Borland tried," she said. "I don't think he was sure about sabotage."

"He was sure. We had found one of the charges."

"Then why didn't the Agency get you out?"

"That's one of the things I want to find out."

"You think the Agency did it? I mean someone at the Agency?"

"Whoever did it knew what he was doing." He put his glass on the mantel. "We should have turned back when we found the first charge. It was jammed behind one of the bucket seats at the wing root. One of the Chinese agents had been sitting on the floor. They preferred the floor. He heard the timer, and he told Jimmy Kao, our Chinese jump master, and we found it. You could hear the timer like a cheap clock.

"The Indian was flying but he came back. It was wrapped up tight in a greasy brown paper, tied with a string, and it was the shape of two sticks of dynamite, maybe three.

"The only way we could have made sure was to open it.

75

But it could have been. booby trapped, so the Indian and I both decided to toss it out. We weren't very smart. We should have looked for another one, because whoever did it didn't take any chances. They made sure we'd go down. They didn't want us talking, either, because the way they rigged it we should have been killed."

He sat down on the coffee table again. "We were just very lucky," he said. "It was a perfect night, a lot of clouds, and you couldn't see a thing. We always flew very low. It was safer. The Migs couldn't find us, and they didn't have time to start anti-aircraft fire. But the Indian and Borland had to dodge the hills—it's hilly country that part of China.

"We had made one successful pickup, and we had to drop a radio set. We got the signal and everything went okay. But it was hard to see, and Jimmy Kao thought the parachute had been a streamer and hadn't opened. There wouldn't be much left of the radio, so we went around again to drop a backup set.

"We had to get it out from behind the jump packs. We took the packs off a partition and shoved them to the side of the cabin. Later, when it was all over, we figured the charge must have been tucked in one of them.

"When it went off, the other packs muffled it, and it just blew the side away. If we had left it on the partition where they'd put it, it could have blown the whole tail off, and we never would have made it."

He stared across the room, remembering. "We were all a little stunned. There was a lot of noise. One of the Chinese was yelling, and the airplane was lurching all over the place and going down fast. Jimmy Kao pulled the jump door so we could get out fast. Those of us who could, got into seats and fastened our belts, and we hit.

"We skidded and then the wing sheered off on some trees, and we spun around, and the plane went up on its nose and slammed into a little ridge. That's what broke Hallee's leg—he was the only one hurt. Someone yelled fire, and the Chinese were screaming, and everyone got out fast."

He looked at her and smiled faintly. "I thought I'd forgotten it," he said.

"Who got Hallee out?"

"Borland and I. That's one of the things I've never been able to figure about Borland. Over there he was a hardhead. When he got back to the States, we figured he would raise hell. But he quit."

"Was Hallee unconscious?"

"We had trouble getting him out. We had to pull him with his leg dragging. He had multiple fractures.

"The Chinese were coming from everywhere. The airplane made a lot of light, and we could see we were right near a bunch of huts or a village.

"Borland and I got Hallee away from the heat, and we were trying to make him comfortable when a couple of local boys with guns came running up, poking the guns at us. Hallee was still out cold.

"The crowd put up a yell. They had grabbed one of our Chinese. Two of them managed to get away, including Jimmy Kao, but they didn't get far. They were picked up the next day.

"The crowd was making a lot of noise, and the plane was still burning. A fat little fellow came along giving orders, and quieting them down. He had two of his militia pointing their guns at us, and I tried to explain to him that Hallee was wounded. Every time I talked to him he'd throw his hands up in the air and yell something. I found out later he was yelling 'Wingpu.' That's where the hospital was. That's where they took us.

"But we had to wait at least three hours before a truck showed up. All we could do for the Indian was to make him comfortable. Borland gave him a shot of morphine from his kit.

"The plane had just about stopped burning, but the Chinese kept coming to look at us. They came all night long, and they'd sit down and stare at us and then after a while they would go away. But the crowd never got any smaller.

"Finally the truck took us to Wingpu. I remember the road wasn't very good, and it took about an hour. We were all shivering. Borland put his jacket over the Indian. Borland was quite a guy in those days.

"It wasn't much of a hospital, a bunch of wooden buildings joined by walkways. They kept us all there, Borland and Roberts and me. They had Hallee in traction for his leg.

"A couple of days later they took us by truck to the outskirts of the town. They had picked up every one of the Chinese agents, and we had to watch them shoot them.

"Hallee was still at the hospital. They were pretty good to him. They had guards at the doors, but they let us visit him every day. They wanted us in good shape for the trial.

"As soon as he was walking around on crutches, they moved us to Peking. They questioned us every day, and they made it clear they wouldn't let Hallee out, or me or Roberts, but they kept hinting about Borland. He was a junior officer and he was in uniform, and they wanted to let someone out for their own propaganda purposes. The Indian figured it was a good deal since they'd convict us anyway, so we signed the papers."

"You mean the confessions?"

"They were just statements of fact. The trial was a lot of nonsense, except they pulled in all the wreckage and pickup equipment, and they had foreign newspapermen there. There wasn't much we could deny. Then they sent us to a prison up north. The Indian had lost a lot of weight. He was still using a cane when he got pneumonia."

"What was the prison like?"

"It was cold most of the time. We had enough to eat, and they would take us out each day for exercise, rain or shine. Even though it was a big prison, we never saw any of the other prisoners, not directly. We even had our own exercise yard. We had a lot of damp, drizzly days, and Hallee started coughing at night. Then one morning he had a fever.

"I remember it was Sunday because Roberts tried to argue with the guards about exercise. We claimed it was a day of rest. But we were forced to exercise and we all got wet. Hallee was shivering. He died a week later, on Saturday afternoon.

"The thing that bothered him most was the airplane. He had a fever, but all that week every time I sat with him he'd talk about finding out who did it. And I promised to find out."

McAlister got up and walked across the room and stared out the window.

She was still sitting with her legs folded under her. "Can you really find anything now?"

"Borland found something when he came back, but they shut him up. I want to talk to Borland. Then there's Gene Cummings. He was running our operation. Before I talk to him, I want to see Martha."

"She's married to him."

"I think she'll help." He smiled. "She was once married to me."

"Does she know you're back?"

"Not yet."

"Your mother is still bitter about her."

"Because she married Cummings. We were all friends in those days. It makes sense. You have to remember they gave me a life sentence. She wrote me once about Borland, and I think she'll know where I can find him."

"Somehow it doesn't seem very important any more."

"Apparently it is," McAlister said. "They don't want me to find out what actually happened. They're trying to stop me."

"Who is?"

"The Agency, the Air Force, too. They've probably got the F.B.I." He looked out the window. "It's peaceful out here, isn't it? That's why you like it so much."

"Yes, it's peaceful. What do you mean, to stop you?"

"It's not really fair to involve you, Ann. But I need to stay here for a few days."

"You know you can stay here. How would they stop you?"

He turned and looked at her. "They don't much care," he

said. "They didn't care about the Indian or any of us over there. I think they know I'm in the States, and they are trying to kill me."

"Oh, Jim, that's horrible," she said. "Are you sure?"

"I'm sure."

"Can't you go to somebody, the police?"

"That's just where I can't go." He turned back to the window and for a few seconds the room was silent. "I know my chances," he said. "It's been a couple of days, and they almost succeeded once."

"That's why you're here."

"I had to run somewhere. I'm sorry."

"Don't be. Why don't you forget the whole thing? You could disappear. You could go back."

He shook his head. "They wouldn't let me go back."

"There must be *something* you can do."

"If I can get the facts out first, before they succeed, then it won't make any difference."

"Won't they come here?"

"Not for a while, a few days. If you'll let me stay here . . ."

"Of course," she said. "But they can't just kill people."

"Maybe not," he said. He was still staring out the window. But I'm frightened, he thought, and it is rather silly for an old man to be scared like a kid.

Chapter  8

"THAT'S a good report," the Director said. "It'll do the trick if he reads it."

"He won't read it," Colonel Rynders said.

He was staring out the car window into the pearly light. They were only a few minutes from the White House, and it was just turning dawn.

"He probably won't," the Director said, "but I told him we'd have a report, all the facts, and this puts it pretty well." He opened the attaché case balanced on his knees, and slipped the report inside on top of his other papers. "Gene Cummings is going to meet you there?" he asked.

Rynders sat back in the seat. The chauffeur was driving fast. "He's been working straight through. He'll be there. I told him General Townsend had been talking to him."

"Damn Townsend," the Director said. "He's got him worried. That's why he had me on the telephone again last night." He snapped closed the locks on the attaché case, one after the other.

Colonel Rynders still had a headache. It had kept him awake most of the night. He took off his glasses. "You know, Sam," he said, "he's our real problem, General Townsend."

"He's the first chairman they've had who understands politics."

"The President listens to him more than State, more than the Agency. We haven't had that kind of general since Marshall and Roosevelt, and Marshall wasn't really political."

"Well, he's gone too far this time," the Director said. "They took a damn strong position against the talks, and it's an obsession with the Old Man."

"I hope you're right," Rynders said. His eye was dry and it hurt, and he wanted to rub it. But over the years he had learned not to. Rubbing made it worse. He said, "Townsend is a lot smarter than most of them."

"He's right about one thing, Ike. The talks fall apart, and it will be a political disaster for the Old Man."

"And the Agency's fault."

"Politically, he's staked everything on it."

"He'll get some kind of agreement, and then he'll claim a success. The newspapers will buy it."

"That's right," the Director said. He put his briefcase down on the floor. "But not if your Chinaman causes problems."

"He won't," Colonel Rynders said. "We'll get him."

"That's what I told him," the Director said, "and that's all you've got to tell him if he comes down for the briefing."

Rynders put his glasses back on. The street was empty, and the car was moving fast, rocking gently. Through the trees he could see the sky touched with pink. Soon the pink would turn baby blue, and they would be at the White House in plenty of time.

"There's always a chance we'll miss," he said.

"We can't afford to miss," the Director said.

"I'm keeping Defense Intelligence in it so they're part of the whole operation."

"You get him, Ike, and I'll take care of General Townsend and the Joint Chiefs and D.I.A., too."

"That's why I've got Cummings running it," Colonel Rynders said softly. "They wanted Cummings, General Whooten wanted him."

"He's pretty close over there."

"He's all right," Rynders said. "He'll keep Defense Intelligence in the picture."

"Not too much."

"He's working for me. He's ambitious."

The Director rubbed his chin. "He wants an embassy, doesn't he? He almost got Ghana after he came back from Defense."

"We couldn't," Rynders said. "He was still working covert. But if these talks succeed, he can have one, and State will go along. He's been surfaced for a long while now, teaching at Georgetown."

"He was over there at Defense for a couple of years helping them reorganize."

"I trained him," Rynders said. "Don't worry about it, Sam. I'll be watching it myself."

"Excuse me, sir," the chauffeur said. "The side entrance?"

They were approaching the White House. "That's right," the Director said. "Lower level, Phillips. We're going to drop off Colonel Rynders."

The car slowed, and they went around the corner past the park. The street lights were still on. They coasted, braked and then swung right to the gate and the little gatehouse.

The guard glanced at the license plates and waved his hand. Hardly stopping, they drove down to the basement garage. Light bulbs were scattered in the shadows. The car swung right and stopped.

"He probably won't show up," the Director said. "If he does, Ike, all you have to do is answer a few questions." He smiled. The President was known for asking questions fast.

"I'll try to keep up with him," Rynders said and opened the door.

"Let me know how it goes. I've got a couple of meetings, but you can leave word with Alice."

"Yes, sir," Rynders said. He got out, carrying his briefcase, and shoved the door closed behind him. He stepped across the sidewalk. The car pulled away behind him, and he opened the door and stepped inside into the light.

There was a desk and a guard in black uniform.

"Rynders," the Colonel said. "Intelligence."

"Morning, sir," the guard said, running down a list. He drew a line through a name. "You know where it is, sir?"

"Yes," Rynders said. "I can find it. Did Mr. Cummings arrive yet?"

"Just a few minutes ago, sir."

He went down the empty corridor under the bright fluorescent lights, his head still aching. He needed some aspirin, but he had put the bottle in his briefcase.

He turned right into the first corridor, found the door knob and stepped inside onto a carpet. The light was softer, and he heard the quiet rattle of teletype machines. There were chairs to his right and another door straight ahead.

A girl was standing with her back to him, short brown hair, brown suit, arranging something on the desk. "Good morning," she said, half turning. "There's coffee inside."

"Morning, Missy," he said, recognizing her.

"Oh," she said, turning, "it's you, Colonel. Mr. Cummings said you might be coming."

"How are you?" he asked. "You still pull early duty?"

"I like it," she said.

She stared at him now with her light blue eyes and her full mouth. For an instant he forgot his headache and the briefing, and he smiled. "Missy," he said, "it's good to see you."

"It's nice to see you, Colonel."

"Is he going to come down?"

"He's here already, but they're working with the map, and that always takes them a long while." She smiled. "Everything has to go on the map."

"Good," he said. "I won't interrupt them." He put his briefcase on one of the black leather chairs. "Can you tell Cummings I'm here?"

"It's all right," she said. "They turn on a light when they finish the military briefing. Would you like some coffee?"

"That would be great."

"Still black?"

He nodded. "I miss seeing you."

"We're living in town now," she said. "The commute is better, and the car picks me up. It's only a few minutes."

"It's been a long while," he said.

"I'll get your coffee." She disappeared through the side door to the teletype room.

What was it Sam was saying the other day? Intelligence is a small town. You spend twenty or thirty years when you can't talk to anyone else, and the only people you know are in the business. Pretty soon you carry the past with you, and you can't leave it. He should have remembered he would see Missy here today.

His head was throbbing. He opened the briefcase, reached into the corner and took out the bottle of aspirin. He poured four pills into his hand, put them in his mouth, and chewed.

What was it, eight or nine years ago, and it had not lasted long. It was after Nakhodka, and even then, with her, he had been awakened at night by the sight of them trying to get back to the submarine. The icy fog was lifting like a curtain and yells issued from the fishing fleet. The gun erupted. Spurts of water, maybe a hundred feet away. The look on their faces when they realized the sub was going, and a bullet hit the young one, Stubbs, and the blood on the yellow, and then he had had to scramble down.

The aspirin tasted sour and flat, and he could feel the grains with his tongue. It was nine years ago.

The door opened and she came back carrying the black coffee. The steam hung in the air above the cup.

There were lines, now, at the edges of her mouth, smile lines. But she was still lovely, and he remembered, suddenly, the way she would wake up after him like a cat, short brown hair hiding her face.

She would sit up and read to keep him company, and then she would fall asleep. He would take the book from her and watch her breathing slowly, her mouth open just a bit. In the morning, he almost always managed to slip away when it was still dark and she was still asleep.

"What?" he said.

"You weren't even listening to me."

"I'm sorry," he said, taking the cup.

"I said they're still working with the map but you can go in if you like."

"I'd rather stay with you." He smiled. "You haven't changed a bit, Missy. You look lovely."

"Thank you," she said. She turned and walked around the desk, putting it between them, and sat down.

"All of you out there," she said. "I suppose you're still working too hard."

"It's my age," he said. "I'm getting old."

"You used to say that years ago."

"Older and wiser," he said.

"I never congratulated you." She picked up a pencil.

"On what?"

"Deputy Director. Jack says you're really running Plans, and I hear all kinds of nice things."

"He's not really supposed to talk about it."

"They've even got a new name for you."

He sipped the coffee. It was very hot. She was doodling with the pencil like a little girl, her head down.

"If I'd been smart I never would have taken it. It's chaos. No more peaceful times."

She looked up. "Poor Ike," she said, smiling. "All of you in Plans, you think that's what you want, but you really don't."

The teletypes had stopped. He could hear voices in the other room. "How are things working out, Missy?"

"I'm happy," she said, "and I think I'm very much in love."

"Jack's doing good work."

"Yes," she said. "Sometimes I worry about you, and I know I shouldn't. Do you know what the men call you now?" Her blue eyes were bright.

"No, what?"

"Maybe I shouldn't tell you."

"I've probably heard it. Anything except the old man. I figure I'm old enough as it is." He nodded toward the inner room. "And that's what they call him."

"They call you 'Fish,' " she said.

He saw that she realized she shouldn't have said it. "I'm sorry," she said.

"It's a good name," he said. "I guess it fits." He sipped the coffee.

"You didn't know it?"

"I've heard it before," he said.

"They mean it affectionately," she said.

"I know." He put the cup down. "How are they doing in there? Maybe I should go in."

"They're supposed to signal me," she said, "so I can check the teletypes. But he never spends more than fifteen or twenty minutes."

"I'd better go in." He picked up his briefcase. "It's wonderful to see you again, Missy. Give my best to Jack."

"Yes," she said, looking down. She pushed a button, picked up the white telephone and said something softly.

Colonel Rynders went past the desk and opened the door.

The map was on the right wall, and there was a young man standing in front of it on a platform, pointing. The President was sitting in one of the white chairs facing the map.

"A minor flare-up there, sir, in the village of Kol-ny, military designation, Unit Four." He touched the map with his finger. There was a big red pin sticking in the spot.

The door shut silently behind him. The briefing room officer was sitting at the desk at the far side of the room. Cummings was getting up from a chair, coming toward him.

"The reports are still confused," the young man said, "but there was a skirmish, and they overran the village."

The President was watching the map. A curtain hung down over the wall, covering a screen for films or slides.

"Five killed, but we don't have a good body count. They had time to take them with them before the gunships got there."

Colonel Rynders could see the pink of the President's scalp. He reached up and stroked the hair at his temple. His black hair was still thick on the sides.

"They took some of our people?"

"Yes, sir, the village elder and his son and a few others."

"We have to stop that kind of thing. They seem to do it at will in that area. Anything else?"

"Yes, sir, a few skirmishes here." He pointed to smaller red pins. "And here, and here. Apparently minor clashes."

"I see. Will you let me have a report on that Two Corps action as soon as possible?"

"Yes, sir."

He was still looking at the map. "Go ahead, Mr. Cummings," he said, getting up. "What about the Menshikov mission?"

Cummings said, "Colonel Rynders is here, sir. He has the report."

"Good," he said, stepping around the chair and looking at Rynders over his glasses.

"Good morning, Mr. President," Rynders said.

He had met him before, but he looked smaller, older, balder in the early morning, as if he had yet to be lifted up by the presidency to look like a President.

"Morning," he said. "I understand we do know something about this fellow."

"We believe he may be a Chinese agent."

The President was wearing a red bathrobe over his shirt and trousers, and the skin of his face was shiny and blue. He must have shaved within the last half hour.

"The whole thing seems rather absurd. General Townsend said they dropped him from the airplane by parachute."

"We know a man dropped from the aircraft, sir, and we think he's an agent. We surmise he used a parachute, but nobody saw him."

"How do you know he was dropped?"

"The man flying escort saw it, sir. Radar confirmed, but we didn't see him open his parachute."

"And this fellow is supposed to be a Chinese agent? Townsend said they had information, some reports, that they were going to bring a Chinese agent into the country."

"Defense Intelligence had the reports, yes, sir. It's our estimate that they were planted."

"Yes, I know," he said. "Lucas informed me. Where did they drop him, Colonel?"

"Near a place called Faysville, sir, in New York. As you know, sir, we believe Menshikov may be totally unaware."

"Yes, I know. Defense Intelligence doesn't agree with you."

"I don't think they do, sir."

"Who sent him then?"

"The KGB, or the military, the GRU. It's our best estimate they leaked those reports. They wanted us to see the drop. They wanted an incident."

"And that would sabotage the talks."

"We think that's what they wanted, yes, sir. It would, if we took official action."

"Lucas said the State Department people agree with you."

"Yes, sir. It's the logical explanation."

"You people are always logical," the President said, turning away and patting the side of his hair. "Even when you are wrong, you're logical, and General Townsend thinks you may be wrong."

"We could be, sir."

"Even if you're right, Colonel, he's here on some mis-

92

sion." He turned again to face the Colonel. "What's your best estimate on that?"

"It could be almost anything to disrupt the talks."

"Yes," the President said. "That's what Lucas said. Even an assassination."

"We don't think so, but it is a possibility." Rynders' head was throbbing.

"And where is this Chinese agent now, Colonel?"

"We're looking for him, Mr. President. We expect to find him, but it may take a day or two. We have a lot of people working on it."

"Do you have any information, any leads?"

"Mr. Cummings is working on some, but nothing definite."

"The fact that they dropped a man is being kept secret."

Cummings said, "The Director put top secret on it, sir. We're moving as fast as we can."

The President looked at him. Cummings said, "With radar, sir, we've been able to pinpoint where he must have landed, and the F.B.I. is combing the area with the local police. Theoretically, they're looking for a man named Lucasta. He's on their wanted list, for murder."

"I want him found," the President said, touching the hair at the side of his head again. "I told Lucas I want you to use all the resources necessary."

"Mr. Cummings is coordinating the search," Rynders said. "Counter Intelligence is working with the Bureau."

"No excuse," he said. "No excuse for an agent getting in that way." He turned to Rynders, peering over his glasses.

"I am personally convinced of the sincerity of Premier Menshikov," he said, "and so is the Secretary of State. Even beyond the talks, Colonel, no one, nothing, must be permitted to destroy the credibility of the Menshikov faction."

"Yes, sir," Rynders said.

"An assassin," he said. "Do you realize what he could do? What does Secret Service say about it?"

"They have some recommendations on security, sir."

"That won't help. One man with skills, and there isn't anything they can do if he is not found. I want that man found, gentlemen. I want him found immediately, and I want to be informed as soon as you have him." He took off his glasses and tucked them in the breast pocket of his bathrobe. "It should not be too difficult if he is Chinese."

"We're not sure of that," Rynders said.

"Absolute priority, Colonel. Premier Menshikov is coming here tomorrow morning. If that man is already in Washington, an assassin . . ."

"Secret Service is covering the Soviet Embassy."

"There are going to be public appearances, gentlemen. We can't hide for two weeks. We can't even tell Menshikov why he should hide."

He was only a few feet away from Rynders, and when he touched his hair, Colonel Rynders saw that his fingertips, with the polished nails, were trembling. "I will not have the talks destroyed."

"Mr. President," Rynders said, "we're doing everything possible. I've covered all the details in the report."

"That's right," he said. "The report." He half turned toward the briefing officer who had come across the room. "Do you have the report, Mr. Timms?"

"I have it, sir," Colonel Rynders said. He put his briefcase on the chair, opened it, and took out the report.

The President looked at the blue cover, stamped "Top Secret." He rolled it into a cylinder and tapped his right leg with it.

"Colonel," he said, "I've spoken before about how important this conference is, not just for the administration but for the nation. I told Lucas last night, we may never have a chance like this again. I want your people to do whatever is necessary to make sure this Chinaman," he waved the report, "this incident does not interfere."

He started toward the door. "It is impossible for me to believe, gentlemen, that all the offices of the Federal government, the Central Intelligence Agency and the Federal Bureau, are unable to locate one man, a Chinaman. I want him found."

He stepped past Rynders and yanked open the door. The bathrobe hung loose down his back. He went out quickly, and Rynders heard the teletypes chattering softly and then the sound of the outer door and silence.

Nobody said anything for a second. "I never saw him like that before," Timms said.

Colonel Rynders took off his glasses. "He's worried," he said. "He's got a right to be worried."

He rubbed his eye with the back of his hand, knowing he shouldn't, but for a second it made the pain go away.

Chapter

9

McALISTER woke up early listening for
the sound of the old lady rattling breakfast pans and the boys
wrestling like puppies, and then he realized where he was.

Gray light filled the room, and the air was cold. She had
put him in the guest room upstairs. A greenish landscape
hung on the wall and near it two small portraits in gold
frames. There was also a large bureau in the room. And on
the floor, leaning against one wall, was his suitcase.

They had had supper, and then they had talked until very
late. He remembered falling asleep once when she was getting some newspaper clippings that she had saved from
many years ago.

He was still tired but he knew that he would not be able
to go back to sleep. He sat up on the edge of the bed and

rubbed his eyes and then his face. His beard stubble was thick. Walking the few steps to the window, he let the shade up. The sky was clear blue. Far away he could see the shadows of the mountains in the distance. There was nothing moving in the valley.

He stood for a minute with his hands on the sides of the window, like a prisoner looking out. He had come a long way to see this, and it was brown and peaceful, as if there was nothing here.

He could see the wide fields, the occasional woods, and the black road like a ribbon. Small shapes far away might be cattle. To the south, he could see the parking lot of the base and two grayish buildings. A tank rose like a balloon on stilts.

From the aerial photographs he knew where the silo was supposed to be. He followed the black road past a big field. There were trees, and he could just make out the dirt road that ran between them. Beyond the trees in the dark brown field was the missile site. He could tell it from the color of the ground. It was shaped like a kidney. A grayish road ran from the trees to its center.

They had briefed him on the missile in Moscow: a three-stage solid fuel rocket with a range of more than nine thousand kilometers, roughly twenty meters long and housed upright in underground silos about twenty-four meters deep and two and a half meters wide. The first operational version had carried a one megaton bomb, about fifty times as much destruction as the famous Hiroshima bomb. But the Minuteman Two carried just about twice as much destructive power, close to two megatons.

They brought the missile in by truck and took it out of the silo for servicing. That's what the road was for. The control cable was buried parallel to the service road. Hermann would be able to work on the cable while staying concealed in the trees.

He would have to go down there. And in a few days he would bring the old man out here and he would be done.

He rubbed his arms. He was cold. He would have a cup of tea before Ann got up. He got into his pants and his shirt and walked in bare feet through the silent house to the kitchen.

It was glistening white and he could smell coffee. There was a note on the table beside the white coffee cup and the plate. He picked it up. It was the same neat hand, like printing, that he had read so many times.

"You were sleeping and I leave early. Eggs in the refrigerator. Please keep Rufus outside. He's not allowed in the house during the day. Only the garbage men and the mailman will come by, and Rufus will bark. I will be home by four o'clock. If you must reach me, you can call the school, tel no. STerling 5-6941. Tell anyone you are my brother. I have a brother. Get plenty of sleep. You need it. Ann."

He had a cup of tea and some breakfast, and then he got his toiletries out of the suitcase and went down the hall to the bathroom. Her stockings were hung neatly over the towel rack. He shut the door, got out of his clothes and looked at his face in the mirror over the sink.

There was blackness all around his eyes, and his cheeks were pale above the beard stubble. She was right; he looked exhausted. He had been running without enough sleep ever since he got on the airplane in Moscow.

It was almost thirty minutes later when he heard the garbage men come and the dog barking. He was in the kitchen. Taking his gun and his topcoat out of the front hall closet, he waited until they had gone before he went out of the house.

The sun was warm, although it was a cool day. He stepped off the porch, and the dog came up with his tail wagging. McAlister patted his head. The birds were making a lot of noise in the trees behind the house. Far off in the valley he could hear a tractor going. The dog was staring up at him with red eyes. He would take the dog with him.

Passing the sign, "Air Force Installation, Winesap II, he turned onto the valley road and headed north, driving slowly. The dog had his head halfway out the side window, poking his nose into the wind.

He caught up with a tractor pulling a rubber-tired wagon. The young farmer was drinking a bottle of orange soda pop as he drove. McAlister couldn't see around him, and he honked. The boy waved him by with the pop bottle.

He went over a slight rise and then past an old, unpainted house off to the left. Ahead he saw another sign and an arrow. It was the Air Force control base.

He drove slowly, looking at the fence and the gray-green buildings and the tank. There was a flagpole, but the flag was hanging down in the still air.

There were some fifteen of these launch control centers scattered over the low hills and the flatland to the north.

99

Each center controlled ten missiles, a hundred and fifty missiles total.

Farther up the valley, he passed fields and a few clumps of trees. On the ridge to the east, he could see Ann's house, its roof flashing in the sunlight.

He watched the road ahead, squinting, and he was almost past the road before he saw it. He backed up. There was a chain hanging between two short posts. A sign read: "No Admittance, U.S. Air Force." The dirt road went straight through the trees.

McAlister twisted in his seat to look back through the rear window. He would have to be careful; it would be stupid to get picked up now. He could come back at night, but he wanted to see the access road in the daylight, and even if someone stopped him, they couldn't be very upset about a man walking in the fields with his dog.

A hundred meters ahead the road curved, and he pulled off onto the left shoulder and stopped. The dog came away from the window and tried to lick his face.

"All right," he said, pushing him aside. "You're going to get out."

He opened the door, and the dog jumped on his lap and then onto the ground. "Crazy dog," he said.

He got out slowly. The dog had already run into the field. They were parked in a little dip. It wouldn't take more than a few minutes, and there was no one in sight.

He took the car keys, slammed the door and slipped under the barbed wire. The pasture had not been plowed for a long time. It was thick with brown grass. The new green was just starting to come up at the roots.

The trees were to his left. He walked a little farther into the field and then turned toward the trees. The dog came running back. Once he was among the trees, no one would see him.

There were only twenty or thirty trees, and it was cooler in their shadows. McAlister headed for the dirt access road. It was just wide enough for a truck, and the dirt had been packed down hard. He could see the valley road behind them and then to the west, just beyond the trees, the missile site in the sunlight.

"Now stay with me, boy," he said to the dog, as he patted his thigh. He followed the road to look out at the missile site.

The wire fence was at least five feet high. There were strands of barbed wire at the top. The fencing ran in a circle attached to posts which were set in concrete, enclosing an area perhaps fifty yards across. The only break in the fence was the gate where the road went through.

The black pole almost the height of a man was the detector. It signaled whenever anything moved on the site. Just this side of it, he could make out the cement silo cap, three yards wide, and painted a dull brown and green to match the ground. There was no indication that anything lay beneath the ground. It might have been a piece of forgotten lawn fenced in by some eccentric landowner, in the middle of nowhere and with no particular purpose.

Two megatons. Enough to wipe out a major city.

McAlister heard something like a truck, and he turned quickly. The dog had drifted off. "Come here, boy," he said, slapping his leg. It was the tractor. He must have stopped somewhere.

He watched the tractor and the wagon go by on the road. Then for a few seconds, standing in the shadows of the trees, he searched both sides of the access road with his eyes. On one side of it they had buried the cables that connected this missile with the launch control center. The surface of a ditch should have settled over the months. But there was no sign of any ditch.

They said the old man could locate the cable; it was the only way to launch the missile. All he had to do was get him out here on the access road close to the missile. If he could stay at Ann's he could bring Hermann here at night without much trouble, and he could work for hours unseen.

The sound of the tractor disappeared up the road. McAlister walked along the road to the chain.

They wouldn't come in by the access road because you couldn't drive past the chain. They would walk in just as he had, over the field. There was no one in sight. He walked along the edge of the road toward the car. His face was glistening with sweat, and he got out his handkerchief to wipe it away.

"Come on, Rufus," he said. "Let's go home."

It had to go some two thousand kilometers, through the atmosphere and back down, and then it would blast a huge crater, churn up dirt, and spread radioactive dust and death. What was it the General said, three hundred people, perhaps more? And he wasn't even sure that Hermann could put it down in that valley.

He reached the car, yanked open the door and got in. He

started the engine but the dog had disappeared. He whistled, as he reached across and shoved the far door open. The dog, who had been waiting there, jumped in and licked his face.

McAlister pushed him aside. "Stop it," he said. "You crazy dog, stop it." He held the dog with one hand and pulled the door closed with his other. Then he pushed down the accelerator and headed back the way he had come.

Chapter  10

H E slept soundly until the late afternoon sunshine seeping in around the window shade began to stir him to consciousness. A cow bellowed in the valley, and halfway between dream and wakefulness he saw himself as a boy, following the cows down the old road, around the swamp and along the creek, just as he had done countless times in his past.

The sun was up and the flies were bothering the cows so that, walking slowly, they swung their tails in self-defense. The brown one with the bones sticking out lowered her head and bellowed.

His mother, in a loose shirt, her long hair twisted into a long braid, was waiting with the gate open as she did each morning, and she put her hand on his shoulder and thanked him.

Then he was on his way back inside the house, and he could smell his father's cigar—the cigar he always smoked first thing in the morning, while he talked about the God-damn railroad.

"Jim," she said. "Jim."

"What?" He awoke instantly, with a start.

Ann was standing in the doorway. "I hate to wake you," she said, "but someone just called you on the telephone."

"What?" he asked, sitting up.

"A man called and asked for you."

"Who was it?"

"He didn't say. He asked for a Mr. Hamill. When I told him he had the wrong number, he asked for you."

"Who'd he ask for?"

"James McAlister. I told him there was no one here by that name, either. But he sounded strange."

"Why strange?"

"After I told him you weren't here, he asked me for the time, London time."

"What did you say?"

"I told him again he had the wrong number. You said they were looking for you, and I didn't know what to do, so I just hung up."

"Good girl," he said.

"It seemed so crazy," she added. Her face was still flushed. She must have run up the stairs.

"It would seem crazy." McAlister smiled and rubbed the back of his neck. "But it's all right, Ann. I think I know who it was."

Since Felix Klass was dead, only the General would know

he might be here. And the General would ask for the time. London was the right city in sequence.

"One of those people from the Agency?"

"He's supposed to be helping me," McAlister said. "There's nothing for you to be frightened about. He'll call back if he wants me. Now let's forget him. I feel like I've slept for a week."

"You still look tired."

"I feel a lot better."

She stepped inside from the door. "If you'll get up," she said, walking to the window, "I'll fix you some orange juice." She pulled the shade, and it rolled up with a snap.

Sunlight poured into the room. She closed the window.

"How was school?" he said.

"I like it, and today things went smoothly enough for me to leave on time. Did you manage to take that walk you mentioned last night?"

"Rufus and I drove through the valley. And I plan to go out again," he said. "I'd like to take you to dinner."

"We are not going to go anywhere," she said. "I'd be too scared to go out, and I picked up a steak on the way home."

"You want to stay here?"

"We can talk. Maybe you won't keep dozing off the way you did last night. It wasn't very flattering."

"I was tired."

"I'm not sure that's a good excuse." She smiled. "I'll get you some juice."

"Do I have time for a shower?"

"Yes, of course. I'll be in the kitchen."

He got up and went down the hall to the bathroom. Shadows still underlined his eyes, and his beard was rough. But he would look a lot better after he had shaved, and the cold water with which he always ended his showers would really wake him up.

A few minutes later, while he was dressing, he heard the dog bark and the sound of a car coming to a stop close by. Ann hadn't said anything about a visitor. He buckled his belt and went to look out of the window.

A black sedan had pulled up on the far side of the road. The door was open, and a squat man was just stepping out. He said something to the driver and then walked halfway across the road and stopped. It was the General.

McAlister had left the .32 in his suitcase where Ann would not see it. But now he took it out and tucked it into his belt. He finished dressing, wearing his suit jacket, buttoned up, to hide the gun. The dog was still barking. He heard Ann's voice.

Through the bedroom window he saw that neither the General nor the dog had moved. Ann was standing beside the dog, holding him by his collar. She was wearing an apron.

Turning from the window, he hurried through the bedroom, down the stairs, and out the front door. The General was shouting something, but with the dog barking his words weren't clear.

"It's okay, Ann," McAlister said, touching her arm. "I know who it is. It's all right."

"Oh," she said. "I can't get him to be quiet." She spoke to

the dog, but he barked again. She patted his head, holding him. "It's all right," she said loudly to the General. "He doesn't bite."

"Splendid," the General said, waddling across the road. "Good afternoon, McAlister. I was afraid we wouldn't catch up with you."

"What the hell are you doing here?"

"I have to talk to you, my boy." He lifted his hat and nodded at Ann. His bony skull glistened for a second. "Good afternoon," he said. "I apologize if I have disturbed you."

"Ann Learson," McAlister said. "This is George Knowles. He's the man who telephoned."

"Quite right," the General said, smiling with his small and perfect teeth. "How do you do. I hope I didn't upset your dog."

"How did you get up here?" McAlister asked.

"Drove up from Denver, my boy. Can we talk for a few minutes?"

"Would you like to come inside?" Ann said.

"That's quite nice of you."

"We'll talk out here," McAlister said. "We'll only be a few minutes."

She looked at McAlister. "Are you all right?"

"Yes," he said. "I won't be long."

"I'll take Rufus. Come on, you," she said, tugging at his collar.

McAlister waited until she had gone most of the way to the porch. Then he said, "You shouldn't have come here."

The General had planted himself like a post on the edge

of the lawn, legs a little apart, hat square on his head, over-coat buttoned despite the warm afternoon sunshine.

He waved his hand in a little circle. "No one followed me," he said. "There is nothing to worry about. I told you I was staying in Denver so I could be of help, and I had to reach you. I called you but no one answered the telephone. I had to find out if you were here. I called again from the crossroads, but the lady hung up on me."

"You take too many chances."

"I take none, my boy. What about her? Is she safe?"

"She's going to help me."

"You have to be sure of her, my boy. Absolutely sure. Everything depends on that."

"She's a friend."

The General shrugged. "You do not have to hurt her, just make sure of her—for your own good, McAlister. When you bring him out here, when you leave."

McAlister said, "You aren't helping anything."

"They expected you back at the hotel, and you did not go back."

"Listen, General," McAlister said, "I told you once before, I don't want you tracking me. I don't want a case officer."

The General dug under his overcoat for his cigarettes. He put one in his mouth. "You were supposed to advise us of your whereabouts."

"I told you to leave me alone."

"We have to take care of you." He lit the cigarette and puffed. "Felix Klass was killed right after your contact."

"I saw him," McAlister said. "It looked like cyanide."

"You saw him?"

"Outside the station." He glanced across the road to the car. The driver was a young man. He had not moved. McAlister said, "Klass and the old man saw you in the station, too."

The General peered at him, his bright eyes half closed in the sunlight. "Ah, I see," he said. "And you thought perhaps we had killed him. You should know better than that, my boy."

"Somebody killed him, either you or the C.I.A."

"I do not think so, not the C.I.A."

"Your people killed him, didn't they?"

"No," the General said. "His death causes problems for all of us."

"Problems?"

"Klass was going to handle Dr. Hermann, and now I have to do that. The old man is difficult and he has his own ideas."

The General might be fat and distasteful, and now he was sweating in his overcoat, but he was no fool and never had been one. The Fat Fox. With Klass dead, there wasn't anybody else to run things.

McAlister said, "Is that what you came for?"

"I must have a date, my boy, a time when you will be finished. I have to make arrangements."

"It's going to be a few days."

"You are being very foolish," the General said.

"Somebody killed Klass, and I'd like to know why."

"There is no time for that kind of thing."

"It's going to take a few days," McAlister insisted.

The General stared at him. "Don't be a fool, my boy. It is simple now. You get Hermann and bring him out here. I am ready to make arrangements for you to go back."

"All I need is an airline ticket, Berlin or Prague, and a contact over there. And I can buy the ticket."

"Of course," the General said. "Of course." He pulled a wrinkled handkerchief out of his pocket and wiped his forehead and his face.

"But they are going to be looking for you, my boy. And that is my job—to get you out—but it will take a little cooperation. Tomorrow, Tuesday, you must tell me the day. I must be prepared."

"I'll tell you as soon as I can."

"We went to a lot of trouble to set up the telephone. It is manned all the time. You let us know soon." He smiled, showing his even little teeth. "You are taking a chance every day you wait."

"You let me worry about that."

The General dropped his cigarette. Smoke curled up from the grass. He stepped on it. "It must be done soon, my boy, and you must cooperate."

"You want cooperation, General, you'll get it. But on my terms. I'll warn you but until then, you stay away. I don't hear from you or see you or know about you. You understand, General? You stay away from here, and from me and from everybody else."

"I am here to help you."

"All right, General," McAlister said. He took his arm and turned him a little. "Now you've had your say. Now you just get back in your car and get out of here."

"We expect you to do the job."

They walked toward the car. "If Hermann is clean, I'll do the job."

"We don't care about Hermann."

"I know. But I do; I'm not going to end up like Klass."

The driver leaned back to open the door. The General shrugged and climbed into the rear seat. McAlister swung the door closed. "Have a nice drive back," he said.

As the engine started, the General stuck his face out of the window. "I say, McAlister, there is something else. Your family is fine. Your wife is getting the letters."

"Stay away from me," McAlister said.

The General sank back onto the seat. The car pulled onto the little road and drove slowly away.

McAlister stood for a minute at the edge of the lawn, looking at the mountains far away, shining white gold in the sunlight. The brown fields had turned almost golden, and the water tank behind the missile base was glistening.

Chapter

11

"WHO is he? What did he want?" Her brow looked full of questions, but her hands were business-like and efficient as she washed a head of lettuce in the kitchen sink.

"He's gone," McAlister said. "I'm sorry, if he frightened you."

She turned off the water and looked at him. "How did he get out here?" she asked. "He even looked evil."

"He isn't very pretty, but he's helping me." McAlister could hear the tension collecting in her voice and see it in her eyes which could no longer directly engage his own.

"All of a sudden everything's gone crazy."

"I shouldn't have come here."

"I didn't mean that." Her lips were trembling. "I'm just

upset. It's so peaceful out here; I never thought anything could change that. But talking about Hallee and that they may be trying to kill you—it's frightened me. I couldn't think about anything else all day." She tried to smile. "I wasn't much of a teacher. Two of the kids asked me what was wrong."

"Maybe we both need a drink," he said.

She nodded, her head down and when she turned toward him there were tears in her eyes. "You could go away," she said. "Some friends of mine have a place in the mountains. They use it for skiing. No one would ever find you."

"You're doing enough for me by just letting me stay here."

"All right," she said, looking steadily into his eyes. Then she saw the gun. McAlister had unbuttoned his suit coat. "You were afraid, too."

"I just didn't want to take any chances," he said. "I wasn't sure who it was until I got out there."

"And you thought it might have been them?"

"I suppose it could have been."

Ann shut her eyes momentarily and then turned to her lettuce, trying to concentrate all her attention upon it and change the focus of her thoughts.

"I have to make a phone call," he said, "and then we'll have our drinks."

He left the kitchen and went upstairs. He hid the gun in his suitcase under some clothes, and then sat down on the side of the bed, checking the airline schedules.

There were a lot of flights from Denver to Washington during the day. He would leave for the airport in the morning, when Ann left for school, and he would have no trouble getting a seat on one of them.

Ann's room was filled with so much late afternoon sunshine that he had to squint to see across its width. The telephone was on the night table alongside her bed. He dialed Operator.

"May I help you?" the voice asked.

"Yes," he said. "I'd like to get the number for Eugene G. Cummings. I think it's Martins Corners, in Virginia. It's near Washington."

"You can dial information directly, sir."

"Would you mind getting it for me?"

"Do you have an address, sir?"

He had to think hard to remember the address. "Tudor Lane or English Lane, something like that." They could have moved. She had written him from that address a year ago, on the baby's birthday.

"All right, sir," the operator said. "I'll try to get it for you."

He heard the operator dialing and talking to information and he waited, listening for the number.

"Operator," he said, "is that the number: Independence eight six two seven one."

"Yes, sir," she said. "Independence eight six two seven one."

He said it over to himself, memorizing it. The operator was dialing. In a minute the telephone would ring.

After almost twenty years he wondered if he would recognize her voice. And would she recognize his? He was going to have to pretend that he was someone else.

He counted the rings, two, three, four, and someone picked up the telephone.

"Hello." It was a female voice.

"Is this the Cummings' home?"

"Who do you wish to speak to, please?" She sounded very young.

"Is Mrs. Cummings there?"

"Who is calling, please?" It could be one of her children.

"This is Albert Hamill," he said. "I wonder if I might speak with Mrs. Cummings."

"Okay," she said. "Just a minute and I'll tell her." The telephone clunked. For a second he heard music.

"This is Martha Cummings."

Her voice had not changed, and it made her image vivid in his mind. He imagined that she was wearing white, a white dress and even white shoes.

"Yes," she said. "Hello." Her voice was very clear.

"Martha." He swallowed.

"Who is this?" she said. "Who is calling, please?"

"Mrs. Cummings," he said, "my name is Hamill, Albert Hamill. I'm calling on behalf of a Mr. James McAlister. He gave me a letter for you."

"What did you say your name was?"

"Hamill," he said. "Albert Hamill."

"Where are you, Mr. Hamill?"

"I'm in New York. I'll be in Washington tomorrow evening if that would be convenient. I promised Jim McAlister I would deliver a letter to you. He was a friend of yours."

"Jim and I were more than friends, Mr. Hamill." Her voice was calm. "Where did you see him?"

"It's all right, Mrs. Cummings," he said. "I'm a Canadian. I saw him over there."

"I see," she said.

"I promised him I'd give you the letter."

"That's very kind of you," she said. "Would you like to come out to the house, Mr. Hamill? We're just outside of Washington."

"Thanks," he said, "but Mr. McAlister didn't want me to mention this to anyone but you. He thought it was rather important not to discuss it with anyone."

"Oh," she said. "Did he say why?"

"Perhaps it was something in his letter."

"I appreciate what you're doing, Mr. Hamill, but my husband and Jim were good friends."

"He wanted me to give you his letter privately. I have carried it a long way."

"Where would you like to meet?"

"He gave me the name of a restaurant called Saverese's on Fourteenth Street. He didn't know if it would still be there."

"Yes," she said. "It's still there."

"Perhaps we could have a drink and dinner."

"How is Jim, Mr. Hamill? Is he all right?"

"He's fine. He's got two boys now and he seems quite happy. We could have dinner and talk about him."

"What time?"

"Seven o'clock, if that's convenient for you."

"I think that will be all right. Seven o'clock tomorrow night at Saverese's. How will I recognize you?"

"I'll find you," he said. "And Mrs. Cummings, you won't discuss it with anyone?"

"No," she said. "Good-bye, Mr. Hamill." She hung up.

He went downstairs and into the kitchen. Ann was still working at the sink. "How about having our drinks out-side?" he said. "I didn't know you had that terrace. It's very nice."

"It's probably a little cold, by now."

"We can try it."

"All right," she said. "You fix the drinks, and I'll finish putting dinner on." She turned and smiled at him. "We'll go outside and freeze."

McAlister sat on the low stone wall at one side of the ter-race behind the house, waiting for Ann who had gone to get a sweater. Rufus pushed against him, as McAlister rubbed his head.

He closed his eyes and thought that, at least, it would be over soon. In just a few days his job would be done, and she would be cursing him and hating him. But he would be gone. He would be back in China.

The door opened. Ann had changed into a white sweater with a high neck. McAlister handed her a drink.

They sat together in silence for a time, and when they spoke, it was of simple things like the loveliness of the val-ley and the sunset, its peacefulness, and the coming of spring. Ann told him about her students, the school, and her neighborhood friends. McAlister sensed that she was relax-ing, the steady flow of words putting her mind at ease.

He had a few important matters to discuss with her, mat-ters that tumbled through his mind now, as she spoke, until they were perfected and arranged into the next steps of his plan.

"Ann," he interjected, "I want you to do something for me."

She looked into his eyes, suddenly forced back into the present with all its uncertainties.

"Yes, Jim. What is it?"

"I have to see some people in a few days. And I would like to meet some of them here." He waited for her reaction. There was more, but he would take his time.

"Certainly, Jim. I want to do anything I can to help."

"It would be a big help." They sat in silence again, each letting the presence of the other temporarily dispel all the fears and worries. Let them go unmentioned, McAlister thought, unmentioned and unrealized. Then he spoke again.

"Can you take some time off in a few days? I would like you to visit my mother, maybe spend two or three days with her."

"I don't understand. Why?" Wasn't he going to be back here then, seeing those people?

"I will be meeting my contacts then—it will be safer if you aren't here. And if someone is looking for me, they will certainly go to my mother's. It would help if you were with her."

"Aren't you going to see her yourself?"

"I don't know if I will be able to. In any case, Ann, it would be safer if you were there."

"Safer for me or for you?"

"Both of us," he said, "and for her."

"Yes, I'll go." She was looking down at her hands now, thinking of Hallee, summoning the same courage she had been asked to summon only once before. It was simple, really, just a matter of accepting the reality of circumstances and doing your best to influence fate. When he had flown that mission over China, he had asked her to accept, and she had. Then she had had to accept the outcome as well. Maybe this was a second chance at triumph.

"I'll have to telephone you," McAlister was saying, "when I know exactly when you should go. And I will buy the plane tickets."

The sun was almost down now, a beautiful star-filled night had spread across the sky.

"And, Ann," he continued, "if anything should go wrong, I want you to contact a man at the Agency—Isaac Rynders. He is an old friend; you can trust him."

In one last effort, she said, "If you trust him, why not call him now, ask him to help you bring your children and Tu-chan to this country."

McAlister answered her seriously. It was something he had thought about long and hard: "I want to go back, Ann. My life is in China."

Chapter

12

IF it is light enough when you get near
Martins Corners, just outside Washington, you can see the
swimming pools behind the houses and the post-and-rail
fences. This is rich and horsy country. The hills roll gently,
and the homes are small estates. Eugene Cummings always
enjoyed driving back to the Corners at dusk.

He liked the road winding through the hills and the sight
of tailored lawns. He liked to take the last curve leisurely and
watch his own wide lawn come into view, stretching gently
upward toward the poplars and the house at the top of the
slope.

The tires skidded on the gravel, as he shot into the driveway. The driveway was bordered by poplars on either side
and curved past a guest cottage that was set back near the

swimming pool and the woods. Then it made a final sharp turn and ended in a wide gravel turn-around. On the right was the barn where Martha kept her horses. The garage was straight ahead, and the door was open.

He braked and coasted in. Her station wagon was there. He shut off the headlights and the engine, and sat for a minute in the dark and silent garage, holding the steering wheel, thinking.

After supper he had to go back to the office to sign the memos that his secretary was typing, and to get the new subversive list from Jake Edwards. It was Cummings' job to select the most likely people for further surveillance. They didn't have the manpower to watch them all.

He shoved open the door and awkwardly forced his six feet of height out of the compact car. He walked around the front of Martha's station wagon, putting his hand on the hood. It was warm. She had not been home long.

Leaving by the side door of the garage, he stopped at the edge of the garden. In the dusk he could see the first sprouts just coming up. They grew vegetables as well as flowers, but he always looked forward with special anticipation to the spring flowers.

On almost every summer morning he would pick a boutonniere, and wear it all day long. But if his luck held, this year they would be leaving to make their residence at an embassy long before the mums came into bloom.

If my luck holds, he thought. He tapped his right fist into his left palm and headed toward the back door. If we get the son-of-a-bitch. It had taken a long time, but at least now he had a commitment. If they got their man, Colonel Rynders would back him and so would the Director who had almost exclusive access to the President's ear.

He let the door shut behind him and walked quietly down the long hall. It joined the foyer at the front of the house. He could hear the television set playing in the children's wing to his left. The children had Thursday supper early.

He put his coat in the front closet, climbed the stairs to the second floor. The light was on in the bedroom, and the door was half open.

He stepped inside. "Martha?"

"Hello, Gene," she called. She was in the dressing room. "Is that you?"

"It's me," he said, thinking who the hell else would it be. There was a black dress on the bed. "Have the children had supper?"

"Yes," she said. "I had Phoebe feed them early. I've got to go out."

She came out of the dressing room wearing her blue housecoat with the high collar. Her reddish-brown hair was brushed, and she had already put on her heels.

"I tried to call you at the office," she said.

"Where are you going?"

"The girl said you had a conference or something and you were going to work late. I didn't think you'd be home for supper."

"I have to go back."

"Cook can fix you something."

"I just want a bite," he said. "I'm going to be busy for a week or so." He smiled faintly and crossed his arms on his chest. "I'm running a special little show."

"Oh?" she said. "Well, I still don't think you should work so late. The children miss you."

She went back into the dressing room. She never asked what he was doing, and in exchange he always told her as much as he could. But she was not very interested in the Agency. She was more concerned about her dinner parties and the children and the horses which she rode almost every morning. The horses were a waste of money, but it was her money, and she had always liked horses.

He tossed his tie and coat on the bed and went to the doorway. She was sitting at the dressing table in front of the makeup mirror with bare light bulbs all around it, brushing her hair.

He said, "It's a special assignment."

"You're not going away?"

"Not out of the country. They need me to run something. I had to get it started the other night."

She brushed her hair slowly and looked at him through the mirror.

He said, "Defense Intelligence had been running it, but Colonel Rynders and the Director insisted the Agency take over. D.I.A. asked for me. I pushed them about the appointment."

"To an embassy?"

He folded his arms again and nodded.

She put her brush down and turned to look directly at him. "Oh, Gene," she said. "I'm so glad."

"They have a number of embassy openings coming up in Africa. Sam Lucas said today that he is sure he can swing it.

He's pretty close in now. The President listens to him on all appointments."

"That's wonderful." She smiled. "I remember how upset you were when they made him Director."

"He was damned hard to deal with when we were reorganizing D.I.A. He tried to dissolve the domestic bureau. That's kind of funny when you think about it, because we're using D.I.A. now, their Counter Intelligence."

She picked up her brush and gave her hair a few more strokes. "This assignment you're doing for them must be difficult."

"They don't have anyone else who can do it."

She put down the brush and examined her lips in the mirror. She found her lipstick. "It's about time, really."

"Yes, it's about time," he said. "Where are you going?"

"Oh," she said. "Mildred Younger." She touched her mouth with lipstick. "She wants to talk to me. She begged me to come out and have dinner with her."

"Have I met her?"

"I don't think so. She's active in the P.T.A. I didn't think you'd be home, and she's got some kind of problem. She wants to talk."

"On Thursday evening?"

She smiled at him. "Husband trouble, I guess. She just wants to have dinner with somebody she can talk to."

"Couldn't she come here?"

"I think she wants to talk where we won't see people."

"Where are you going to meet her?"

"You're like the F.B.I. tonight."

"I don't mean to be," he said.

"Darling," she said, "would you mind getting me the dress from the bed?"

He turned from the dressing room and got the dress. When he came back she had shut the door half way; she didn't like him to watch her getting dressed. He handed the dress through the opening, and stood outside the door.

He said, "What's her husband's name?"

"Ernest," she said. "Ernest Younger. They live over on South Woodbine."

"You have to be a good Samaritan?"

"I guess somebody has to be." She opened the door and turned her back to him. The dress fit her well, and it made her appear a little thinner and a little taller than she really was. "Can you do the snap for me," she asked, "at the top?"

He snapped it. "I wish you weren't going out," he said.

"Well, I wish I wasn't, too. But I'll be home early, darling, probably before you."

She went back into her dressing room and came out with her pale yellow spring coat. He helped her put it on, and then she kissed him quickly on the cheek. "Have the cook fix you something," she said.

She started out of the bedroom and stopped. "Oh, Gene," she said. "I'm really very happy about the appointment. It's wonderful, darling. You've been working for it for so long."

"Have a good time," he said. Through the window he watched her cross the lawn and enter the garage. She was walking fast, almost running.

He stood there for a long while, a big man with his arms folded on his chest staring into the dusk. He had been in the

Agency for many years, and he had learned to trust the gentle stirrings of his subconscious mind. He knew that something was wrong.

There was a white telephone on the table beside the bed. He got the directory out of the drawer and looked up "Younger, Ernest." Then he dialed.

The telephone rang a few times, and a man answered. "Hello?"

"Hello," he said. "Is Mrs. Younger there, please?"

"Who is calling?"

"This is Gene Cummings," he said. "My wife was going to meet Mrs. Younger, and I wanted to reach her."

"How are you?" the man said. "This is Ernie Younger. Mildred's right here now, let me ask her." He put the telephone down.

Cummings waited.

He came back on the telephone. "I'm sorry," he said. "I guess there's been a mixup. Would you like to speak to Mildred?"

"She's not expecting my wife?"

"There was some kind of P.T.A. meeting scheduled but it was called off last week."

"I see," Cummings said. "Thanks very much. If you should hear from my wife, would you be kind enough to ask her to call home?"

"Certainly," Younger said. "I'll tell Mildred."

"Thanks," he said. "Thanks very much." He put the white telephone back on its cradle.

Cummings followed the dark hall down the stairs and into the east wing, through the dining room and the breakfast nook, past the children's bedrooms and into the rumpus room. The light was on, and the television set was blaring.

Liza was sitting crosslegged on the floor reading a book and watching television at the same time. Her long dark hair was touched with red like her mother's. It hung loose below her shoulders. The two little ones, dressed in their pajamas, stared open-mouthed at the screen. Phoebe was sitting on the couch, watching the program, too.

Liza said, "Hi, Dad," and went on reading.

Little Harry and Nancy jumped up and ran to him, arms high, yelling, "Daddy, Daddy, Daddy!" He gave them each a hug.

"What are you watching?"

"It's just a cartoon, Daddy."

"Come on," Liza said. "Don't make so much noise. I can't read."

Nancy gave his legs a second hug. Then the television reclaimed their attention and both children walked slowly back to their seats on the floor. Nancy had her thumb in her mouth.

Cummings patted Liza on the head and stepped past her. "Hello, Phoebe," he said. "Are they being good kids?"

"Oh, yes, sir," she said, smiling. "They're almost always good."

"Did Mrs. Cummings tell you where you could reach her?"

"She said you would be at the office, but she gave me a number, too. I think I wrote it down somewhere."

"I want to call her," he said. "Do you think you could get it?"

"Now let me see if I can find it," she said, getting up. She went across the room. Her bedroom was at the end of the hall just beyond the children's rooms.

It was a few minutes before she came back, and then she was holding a little piece of paper torn from a sheet.

"The telephone number?" he asked.

"No, sir," she said, peering at the paper. "She just told me the name of the restaurant. Something like Servers or Saveres."

He stared at her for a fraction of a second. "Saverese's," he said. "Is that it?"

"Yes, sir, that's it." She smiled. "I never heard of it before."

"It's a restaurant downtown," he said. He walked past her to the door. "I'll probably have to go back to the office, Phoebe. If you see Mrs. Cummings later, will you tell her that?"

"Yes, sir, I will," Phoebe said.

He said good night to the children and walked through the house to the study where he had his desk. Martha called it the library because two of the walls were covered with bookshelves, but it was his room. He kept the family accounts in the file. His shotguns were in the case behind the desk. His fishing equipment, the old shooting jacket with the red panel in the back, his waders, and his winter boots were in the big closet.

He sat down at the desk and folded his arms. After a moment, he pulled out the top right drawer and reached far into it past the pencils, pens, loose paper clips, the Scotch tape, and the stapler. The gun was wrapped in a rag. He yanked it out.

It was a .38 automatic. The hammer release was shaved and the mechanism reworked so that when you pulled the trigger and held it, the gun fired all eight rounds in a spray.

When they had been roommates, they had gone there often. It had been McAlister's favorite restaurant. Even after McAlister married Martha, and they had taken over the apartment, he and Jim Thomas sometimes would meet them at Saverese's. On Friday nights they had a piano player who played songs, and everyone would sing. That was a long time ago.

He snapped the gun's release and caught the magazine as it slid out of the butt. He put the gun down, tossed the magazine into his left hand and reached quickly into the drawer again. The box of rounds was way inside. He shook it open and spilled the rounds on the desktop.

McAlister had been over there for many years, and D.I.A. was right. They had sent him back.

Quickly, using his thumb, he slid the rounds into the magazine, and shoved it into the butt. He got another magazine out of the drawer and loaded it, too.

McAlister had married a Chinese girl, and they had had a long time to work on him. But it didn't seem possible he would be such an ass. He was a damned fool, working for them and seeing Martha. And it could ruin everything for Cummings.

He shoved the gun and the extra magazine into his pocket and went slowly down the hall.

13

McALISTER backed carefully into the first space he found. It was a few cars down from the well-lit parking lot entrance and would afford him a clear view of each car that came in, as well as the driver. By looking between the parked cars, he could also watch the front of the restaurant.

He had rented the car at the airport, using his credit card and operator's license in the name of Hamill. It smelled new and probably was. The speedometer registered only eight hundred and thirty-six miles. He settled back in the seat to wait.

For a long while there was no sign of Martha, and he was starting to worry when he saw the station wagon swing a little too fast into the lot and slow.

She was alone, sitting calm and straight. He recognized her as much by the way she sat as by her looks. She drove past him into the lot hunting for a place to park.

McAlister shoved open the door and watched her cruise to the end of the lot and then pull in among the cars. The headlights went off. Making his way between the parked cars, he stepped onto the sidewalk. He would encounter her here, under the light from the buildings, where she could see him clearly, and would surely recognize him.

Her car door slammed, and she left the parking lot, following the sidewalk toward him. Her pocketbook swung gently with each even step. McAlister waited.

She was almost past him when she chanced to glance up momentarily. She stopped short, her eyes wide with a mixture of fear and disbelief.

"It's all right, Martha," he said. "It's me. It's Jim."

"Jim?" she said. "Good Lord! I thought it was your voice but I couldn't believe it."

His eyes and the pull of years drew her to him. He put his hands on her arms and held her. "Let me look at you," he said. "You haven't changed."

"Have they let you out, Jim? Are you back for good? Why didn't you write? Why didn't you tell us?"

"It's complicated," he said, looking beyond her. An open convertible was coming into the parking lot. "Did you come here alone?"

"You told me to. I even had to lie to Gene." She smiled. "Oh, Jim, Gene will be so delighted."

"How is he?"

"He's fine, fine. But there hasn't been anything in the newspapers."

"Nobody knows I'm here."

"How about your children, your family? Are they with you?"

"I came alone," he said.

"Oh." She was struggling against the realization that Jim's return might not be as simple, forthright, and permanent as she wanted it to be.

"Let's get a drink," he said. He took her arm, and they walked together toward the entrance to the restaurant.

"Why don't we go right out to the house? We can probably catch Gene."

"I can't do that," McAlister said. He stopped and looked at her, seeing for the first time the lines in her face and forehead.

"Martha," he said, "I'm here for just a few days. They haven't let me out. I have to go back. I came to you because I knew I could trust you."

"Back to China? They can't make you go back."

"My family's over there."

"Why don't you contact the Agency? They could help you."

"I don't have much time, and there are some people I have to see. The Agency would want briefings—it would take a week. You know the Agency. They'd try to salt me away for days."

"But you could see Gene."

"Not now," he said. He touched her arm reassuringly. "In

a few days, I'll see him, and I want to see Isaac Rynders. Is he still running things?"

"He's a Deputy Director."

"Let's go inside. We can talk over drinks."

Saverese's had changed. Its casual, lively atmosphere had been replaced by a dignified quiet, and they had added another room.

At the bar, three men were talking. A young couple occupied one of the small tables near the wall, but the rest were vacant. Martha sat down at the nearest one, slipped out of her coat, and put it over the back of her chair.

In the soft light, the lines disappeared from her face, and her reddish hair shone in waves just as if twenty years had not really passed at all.

"I've only been here a few times," she said. "Gene and I came for dinner years ago."

"I was afraid they'd gone out of business."

They ordered drinks and talked for a few minutes.

"It brings back memories," she said. "It's almost as if we were both working at the Agency again."

"Yes," McAlister said. He watched the bartender fixing their drinks. She had been a research assistant then, young, and very attractive, and they had come here for dinner on the weekends when the restaurant employed a piano player.

"How do you like living in Washington now?" he asked.

"It's very normal. Except for Gene's work, it's not very exciting." She looked at him. "You used to talk about leading a normal life."

He lifted his drink in the air. "It didn't work out that way," he said.

"Do you *want* to go back, Jim?"

"I don't have any choice."

"What is your life like there? Are you content?"

"It's a lot better than the propaganda would have it. There are a lot of luxuries we don't have, but we have all the essentials. We're raising two healthy boys, and I'm doing something I enjoy. As soon as they found out I had a degree they sent me back to school. I'm working as a chemical engineer, and I like the work."

"And your wife?"

"She's an engineer, too. She runs part of a tractor factory."

"She sounds very brilliant."

He smiled. "She's a better engineer than I am. You'd like her." He looked at her for a minute. "Martha," he said, "do you remember when the plane went down?"

"Yes, of course."

"Everybody said it was ground fire. It wasn't. Somebody put plastic or T.N.T. aboard with a timer."

"That's what the Chinese claimed."

"They were right. You remember Borland, the copilot. He knew when he came back. He was supposed to get us out. But he didn't."

"You think someone stopped him."

"I want to ask him about it before I talk to anyone at the Agency, even to Gene. You wrote to me about Borland."

"Yes," she said. "I saw him last year, at a party here in Washington, and we talked about you."

"Can you remember where he lived?" he asked.

"I remember we talked about horses. . . . Yes, he used to

135

live on Long Island, but he flies for one of the airlines and he had recently moved to Connecticut."

"That's good enough," McAlister said. "I can find him."

"Gene said that it was ground fire, and that you signed those confessions because you had to. He said they used torture."

"They didn't have to use torture. The Agency may not admit it, but I think they know there was an explosive aboard the airplane."

"Why don't you just ask Gene?"

"I will," he said, "in a few days. But once I talk to Gene, the Agency will want me for days, for the China section."

He smiled and looked at her for a minute. He was not sure that she understood or that she cared very much. She had not changed. He should have realized that she would not know anything. Cummings never told her anything. And she never tried to find out. After the plane went down she probably had cried a little, but her nature is practical, and she has a talent for bouncing back. Cummings was standing right there beside her, so she married him.

He said, "Martha, I need two days, maybe three. I don't want Gene or the Agency to know I'm back until after I've talked to Borland. It may not seem important to you, but it is to me."

"You want me to keep it a secret?"

"For a few days. Can I depend on you, Martha?"

"All right, Jim. Yes."

"I'll be back in Washington then, and we'll all get together."

"Come for dinner," she said, "and I'll ask Rynders if you like. How about next week?"

"Fine," he said. "Let's make it next Wednesday. Unless I call you."

They sat in silence for a few seconds, and then McAlister got two menus from the serving table at the end of the bar. On his way back to their table he looked cautiously around the dining room. Saverese's was still doing a good business. Most of the tables were full. There were no single men strategically placed. The waiters in their red jackets moved quickly and gracefully.

He said, "How about some dinner? If I remember correctly, the food here was pretty good."

The food was still good. While they ate he told her about the first prison and the hospital, the show trial, and then the long, cold days in the little cell, the days that turned into weeks and months. They had sentenced him to forty years. For a man in his twenties, forty years were an eternity.

He described solitary, the living death when you can do nothing but sit on the side of the cot and stare into space. But anything is better than nothing, and eventually you reach the point where you would do anything they want you to.

You sign anything because nothing could be worse. Both he and Roberts had signed paroles and had agreed to study. Then everything changed. They gave him books, pamphlets and newspapers they wanted him to read, and then one day, as if they had just realized he had a chemical engineering degree, they asked him if he would like to go to school, learn

Chinese and work as an engineer. They gave him special language classes and they sent him to the university. And he had learned and, perhaps, changed. Three years he spent at the university, studying and working in the laboratory, and then teaching. Finally they assigned him to a design and construction group to build a small acetic acid plant in the northeast. When that was completed, they sent him to Liutsing to build an organics complex. It was there that he met Tu-chan, and that had changed him, too, so that he was less American and more Chinese and still a combination of them both.

Martha talked about her children, and about the days when she was first alone. And then they planned the imaginary future when he and Tu-chan might visit halfway around the world. It was late when he paid the check and helped her on with her coat. He followed her outside. It had become much colder.

"Come on," he said, taking her arm. "I'll take you to your car."

She said, "Gene will be furious when he finds out."

"I'll tell him it was all my fault."

"He'll be furious because I didn't tell him."

He smiled at her. "By then it won't make any difference."

They walked through the almost empty parking lot and stopped in front of her car.

"I'll call you in a few days," he said.

"Anyway," she said, "it's good to have you back."

"It's good to see you again."

She leaned forward and kissed him lightly on the lips.

"It's good to have you back, even if I have to keep it a secret."

He opened the station wagon door for her. She slid into the seat. McAlister shut the door, turned, and began walking across the lot, toward his rented sedan. He glanced at his wristwatch. Ten-fifteen. He had to spend the night somewhere, and then contact Borland. A couple of telephone books would find him. He could fly to New York and stay at a hotel near the airport.

He heard the car before he saw it. The engine was racing. For a fraction of a second he wondered why she was starting her car in such a rush, and then he realized that it was not Martha's car coming toward him.

He glanced left.

It was black and shining and it had no headlights and it was coming too fast for him to escape. The front would hit him and the flat, pale windshield.

He twisted, trying to get out of the way, but his legs wouldn't move fast enough. His feet seemed rooted to the ground.

But he was flinging himself backward, when the car hit him.

It slammed into his side, and he was still twisting. He threw his hands ahead, trying to break his fall as he went down. The car roared away. His left hand hit and scraped, and then his head struck the pavement. He tried to hold himself up off the pavement but there was pain in his hip and side where the car had hit him, and he couldn't manage.

"Jim, are you all right? Are you okay?"

His face was on the ground. He shoved himself up a little, fighting the pain in his head.

"Don't get up," she said. "Wait until I get some help."

He shook his head. "No," he said. "It's all right. I'm okay. Nothing broken. I'll be all right." He rolled a little and sat up.

She was crouching beside him.

There was a pain in his side, and his head ached. He could have been killed.

"I'll be all right," he said.

He heard footsteps and voices. Someone was running from the restaurant. There would be a crowd, and that wouldn't do. Even a small crowd would bring the police.

A man said, "Is he okay?"

"He shouldn't move," Martha said. Her voice was firm and calm.

"It's all right," McAlister said. "Did you see the car, Martha?"

"He was going too fast. By the time I heard him and turned around he had gone. I was just starting to back out."

McAlister pushed himself up. Someone behind him took his arm and helped him stand. "Thanks," he said. His head throbbed. "I'm all right now," he said. "He was coming so fast I never saw him, but he missed me."

"Crazy bastard," someone said.

"You sure you're all right?" It was a big man wearing a tuxedo jacket, a headwaiter.

"I'm okay," he said. His head hurt. He wanted to close his eyes and hang onto something, but he had to move now before a crowd gathered. The pain would go away eventually.

He had been wrong. He had figured the Russians or the Agency had killed Klass. But he had been wrong because they would never try to stop him like this, not now, not here. They'd be more efficient.

The man in the tuxedo said, "Maybe you should come inside and lie down."

"I have to make a plane," McAlister said. "I'm all right. The car didn't hit me. I'd just like to be left alone."

Someone walked away from behind him. His side still hurt. He put his hand on Martha's arm. "Just walk with me for a minute." They started toward his car.

He said, "Did you see what kind of car it was, who was driving?"

"I didn't get a look at it."

"You came alone, didn't you, Martha? You said you came alone."

"I didn't tell anyone."

"It was probably a drunk," he said. "An accident."

"Are you sure you're not hurt?"

"Sure," he said. He stood up straight. "It had to be some drunk or a nutty kid or somebody in a hell of a hurry." He smiled.

"You scraped your hand."

"I'll wash when I get to the airport."

"Maybe I should drive you."

"I'm fine," he said, "believe me." His head still ached, but he leaned over and kissed her cheek. He could smell her perfume, the same perfume she had worn twenty years ago. "Now you go," he said. "I'll see you and Gene in a few days."

"Good night, Jim," she said. He watched her walk away, her steps loud in the empty lot. Her hair glistened in the light. She did not look back.

He got into the car and sat with his hands resting on the steering wheel. The headlights of her car went on and then the station wagon backed out of its space. He watched her until she had driven past him and onto the highway, satisfied that she was safely on her way.

McAlister touched his belt. The .32 was still there. So was his headache and the pain in his side, and his left hand hurt every time he moved it.

It could have been an accident, a drunk or a kid, but it might have been intentional. The car didn't have its headlights on. But the Agency wouldn't try to run him down with a car.

He started his car, turned on the headlights and drove slowly out of the lot. His leg was twitching. He put the heel down hard so he could press the accelerator evenly, and then swung onto the highway.

Chapter

14

IT was a little after eleven o'clock when Martha Cummings got home. She drove around the last long curve east of Martins Corners, and when the wheels rumbled on the washboard bumps in the road, she knew that she was almost there.

She had been driving slowly all the way, chewing her thumbnail, thinking and worrying, which was not like her. But if Gene were waiting for her, she would have to lie again, and she did not look forward to this.

She let her hand drop to the wheel. The car came out of the curve, and the headlights shone on the gray mailbox ahead on the right. Beyond that, the empty black road ran on into the darkness. She touched the brake and slowed going past the mailbox. The tires crunched on gravel as she entered the driveway.

Gene's black car was hardly visible in the darkness of the garage. At least he was home. Sometimes, when he worked late, he spent the night at the office, then called in the morning at breakfast time.

She sat for a minute, sorting out her thoughts. It had been nice to see Jim. He had gotten older, but he really hadn't changed even after all the years. She had forgotten how much she had once loved him. Twenty years ago? It was difficult to believe.

Outside the garage, the night air was cool, and she could smell the wetness of spring. She looked at the dark house. The children would be asleep, Nancy, and Howard with his arms flung everywhere, and Liza who was twelve and not a child anymore. At the far end of the house she could see the yellow light in the bedroom window. Gene was still awake.

Thank God for the children. There wasn't much else now. She had gone away twice last year just for the sake of sanity, but she had always come back early because of the children. Carefully, with the flat of her hand, she pushed her hair back on the right side. She had told Jim that she was happy. What else could she have said?

She crossed the gravel driveway, listening to the crunch of her own steps until they disappeared on the brick path to the back door. She stepped inside. The house was silent. She walked softly down the hall and up the stairs, and then she could see the yellow light at the far end of the wing. When she pushed open the door and stepped inside, she saw Gene sitting on the divan, staring into space, a drink placed conveniently on the table beside him. He looked very big in the lamplight.

"Hello, darling," she said gently. "What are you doing?"

"Sitting," he said. "Thinking. You're late."

"I couldn't help it," she said. She could smell the scotch.

"Do you want a drink?" His voice was monotone, flat.

"No thanks," she said. "I'm rather tired."

"What took you so long?"

"I hurried as fast as I could." He wasn't really angry, she thought. It was just the light. It made his mouth seem hard and his nose thin like a knife.

"How was Margaret Younger?" He picked up the glass from the table.

She didn't want to talk about Margaret Younger. She slipped out of her coat. "Have you been home long?" she asked, going past the side of the bed and into her dressing room.

She had left the top off her perfume bottle. That was stupid, and it wasn't like her. She had been in too much of a hurry. She replaced the cap, carefully hung her coat in the closet, and then stepped out of her shoes. She was rummaging through the closet for her robe when she heard Gene's voice. "Did you say something?" she asked.

He was standing just outside the door of the dressing room. "Martha, would you like a cup of tea?"

"Oh, yes," she said, feeling reassured. Everything was going to be all right. The tea was a ritual. "I'd love a cup, Gene, but I'll fix it. Just let me change."

"That's all right," he said. "I'll be right back."

She knew what would happen, and that was the nicest part, anticipating. He would come back with the tea things on the silver tray. The tea would be in her favorite cup with the rosebuds, steaming hot, and it would be fragrant with lemon. They would talk for a few minutes, and he would drink only half a cup because he didn't really care for tea. Before she finished her cup, he would touch her hand or kiss the top of her head or get up and turn out the big light by the divan and then he would gently drop the robe from her shoulders.

She chose her dark green robe, the one he liked best. It was going to be all right. He really hadn't doubted her story about Margaret Younger. She had been silly to worry.

Pulling the bathrobe belt tight, she went into the bedroom to wait. It was the nicest room in the house—and her favorite—with the desk that had been her mother's, the divan, and the little marble-top table shaped like a barrel. As a child she had often pretended she was a queen and that table would be her throne. Her father had been an ambassador to Peru and to Colombia before he went back to the law firm. The table was one of the things they had always taken with them, wherever they were living.

She walked around the bed and stood at the picture window. She would miss this room and the house, if they went overseas. They could take the furniture, at least some of it.

She heard Gene's footsteps and turned as he came through the door. He was walking carefully, with the tea things on the silver tray.

"The tray looks lovely."

"Just for you," he said. He set the tray on the table. "I was worried about you tonight."

"You shouldn't have been, darling," she said as she poured the tea. It was a little weak.

He took two sugars, then he said, "How was Margaret Younger?"

"Talkative," she said. "I came home as quickly as I could." For a few seconds the room was silent. She said, "I'm going to miss this room. It's the nicest room in the house." She smiled at him. "I hope we have a large bedroom overseas."

"I thought we'd keep the house here. We'll just close it up." He sipped the tea, still looking at her.

Martha pushed back her hair with her right hand.

The room was quiet again. She poured a little more tea into her cup. It was dark. After a minute, looking down at the tea, she said, "Why don't you turn out the light?"

"That's a good idea." He walked around the divan and turned off the standing lamp. The room was dim with only the light beside the bed burning.

"That's better," he said.

She nodded in agreement.

"Have you finished your tea?" He was still standing.

She saw him watching her, his eyes gray and bright with their own light. Rising, she stood before him, offering her hand. Pulling her toward himself he could feel her body beneath the green robe. They kissed and the robe fell to the floor. He led her to their bed.

She felt his weight upon her and the strength of his desire, her own passion rising to his. With her eyes closed, everything was forgotten except the pleasure of the moment. And then he stopped.

High above her, he was holding himself up with his arms

straight. Suddenly, because he did not move, she knew something was wrong.

She caressed his back. "Gene, what is it?"

He was staring at her. "I want you to tell me something."

"Yes, of course, darling."

"Whom did you see tonight?"

"What?" she said.

"You didn't see Margaret Younger."

"Oh," she said. "Please, Gene. Can't we talk about it later?"

"No," he said.

He peered down at her in the dim light like a huge bird with a sharp beak. He was going to peck at her. She turned her face away.

"No," he said. "Look at me." A hand pushed against her cheek. The gray eyes stared without blinking.

"Please, Gene," she said. In a minute she was going to cry, and she did not want that.

"I want to know what happened, Martha. You didn't see Margaret Younger but you saw someone else."

"Gene, let me up, please." She put her arm up across her face, trying to stop the tears.

"I want an answer," he said.

She twisted, but he was immovable and cold, like something foreign. And he frightened her.

"Where is he now, Martha?"

With an angry movement, she freed herself and quickly sat up on the edge of the bed, her arms covering her breasts. Gene had gotten up too, and now he was behind her. "Where is he now?" he repeated.

"That was you," she said, whispering, "that was you in the lot."

"Where is he, Martha? What hospital?"

The tears were streaming down her face—fear, humiliation, confusion. She wanted her clothes. She rose.

He was standing in front of her. "Sit down," he said.

"My robe."

"I said sit down." He grabbed her arm and pushed her backward.

"You've always been secretive, but I thought you had more sense."

"Let me alone," she said. She couldn't stop the sobs, as if it were someone else crying.

"Jesus Christ," he said. "McAlister. He's working for the Chinese, and you meet him. You're out of your mind."

"Let me alone."

"I've left you alone too much. Why didn't you tell me he was here?"

She looked at him through her tears. "He didn't want you to know he was back."

"The son-of-a-bitch," he said, slamming his fist into his left hand. "That proves he's working for them."

"But you were friends."

"You little ass," he said angrily. "You know there's something wrong when he comes back here, now, after all these years." He turned away, walking across the room.

"You've gotten yourself into the middle of an operation. People get killed in these things. He's working for them, and you go and meet him."

"He was once my husband," she said. "He wouldn't hurt

me. And he doesn't have anything to do with the Agency. He was in prison over there."

"He's been out for years. We had information he was coming."

"I don't believe it."

He turned on her. "Why do you think he came here? To have dinner with you? What business do you think we're in?"

"He's not in it and neither am I."

He bent over her, his eyes bright. "Oh yes, you are. You're my wife, and you've gotten yourself in it, Martha, right in the middle. And now you're going to help us get him."

"I won't."

"You'll do what I tell you. You're my wife, Goddamn it."

"You tried to run him down." She dropped her face into her hands. "You tried to kill him."

The bitch. She had lied from the beginning. Maybe she had always felt that McAlister was something special, even after their own marriage. The bastard was back now, and if anybody knew she had seen him, it could ruin everything.

"Where is he?" he said.

"I don't know. He was going to catch an airplane."

"He wasn't hurt?"

"Your car missed him."

He turned and slammed his fist into his palm. Goddamn it, he thought, I was sure I got him. I heard the fender hit. It should have put him into the hospital where we could pick him up.

He grabbed her hair and twisted so that her face turned

upward. She gave a cry of pain, lifting herself, and she was looking up at him.

His mouth was open, his nose like a beak. "Where did he go?"

"I promised I wouldn't . . ."

"Where is he, where, damn it!" She had no business not telling him. She had no right to make him hurt her. She had no right.

She saw his right hand raised and he yanked her hair brutally.

"All right," she said, her voice a whisper. "Stop it. I'll tell you."

He let go of her hair, and looked at her in the dim light, head down, hair falling over her face, the hunch of her shoulders and her folded arms protecting her breasts. She was old, old and naked, and he wanted to hit her. But it wouldn't do any good now. She was frightened, and she would talk.

"Where did he go, Martha?"

"He didn't tell me," she said. "I swear I don't know."

"All right then, what did he want?"

"I promised," she said. She looked up at him and rubbed her nose with the back of her wrist. The tears had stopped.

"You promised," he said, turning away. "He comes back after more than twenty years, and he's working for the Chinese, and you promised."

She saw that he was afraid, pacing, slamming his fist into his hand. "Don't yell," she said. "You'll wake the children." She stood up.

"Damn you," he said, staring at her.

She was sitting up straighter. She pushed back her hair. He could see that she wasn't afraid any more, as if she knew for certain that he would not hit her.

She got up and stepped past him to pick up her robe.

"All right," he said. "What did he want? He wanted something."

She put on the robe and she turned. "He asked me about the airplane."

"What airplane?"

"The one that went down in China. The one they were on."

He was surprised. "What did he ask about?"

"He said the airplane was sabotaged. He thought I might know something about it."

"They were shot down by the Chinese."

"He said they weren't."

"They wouldn't send him over here for that."

"Well, that's what he asked."

"What else did you talk about."

She pulled the robe tighter about her. "We talked about you," she said, "and the children and his children. He has two boys. Yes, that's all. Now if you don't mind, I'd like to wash up and go to bed."

"What else, Martha?" He grabbed her arm, gripping it so hard it hurt. "Don't play games with me," he said.

"Let go of me."

"What else did he want?"

She said, "He wants to see someone."

"Who?"

"He asked me to set up a meeting with Isaac Rynders."

"Why Rynders?"

"He didn't tell me," she said softly. "Why don't you ask Rynders?" She started toward the dressing room.

"Where's the meeting going to be?"

"I'm going to ask Rynders about it. He will call me and tell me what to do."

"When?"

"In two days." She stared at him. "For some reason he doesn't trust you, Gene. But I believe him, and I'm going to call Rynders. It's the least I can do."

"No," he said, "no, Martha, you'll do what I tell you and you won't talk to Rynders. I will. We'll set up a meeting."

"What do you mean?"

"You're going to help. You'll tell him where to meet Rynders."

"I won't," she said.

He stared at her for a minute, not moving. He said, very softly, so it was almost a whisper, "Yes you will."

His gray eyes stared deeply into her. "Take off that robe," he demanded.

"You can't." Defiantly, she pushed her hair back from her face. There was a bruise on her cheek.

He went to the bedside lamp and turned it off. She thought of running to the bathroom but he was already in the way. She could see his form in the dimness.

"You can't," she said. "I'll scream."

He grabbed her arm and pulled. She tried to keep standing but he was too strong. She fell to the floor on her knees. He fell on top of her, throwing her down. She tried to turn away, swinging to one side.

His hand pushed her face. His leg split her knees apart. He shoved his wrist against her neck, pressing. She was choking. She couldn't talk. She flung her head from side to side.

He was saying something, but she couldn't hear, and she tried to twist her hips, her legs. But it was no good. He was there, pressing her down.

When he entered her, she twisted again and then collapsed. She could hear herself moaning as the pain consumed her.

Chapter

15

AT that time of the year in Easton, Con-
necticut, it is just turning dusk when the men get home from
the city. The children have not yet been called in for supper,
and those who live around the Charles Street hill stay out
playing and riding their bikes. They like to race out of the
driveways and coast down the long slope.

Charles Street dead ends at the top of the hill where the
land flattens out. Number Eighteen is near the top, and
McAlister had just passed it when he noticed the number on
a fence post. He continued around the circle and then pulled
up beside the fence. Sidney A. Borland's house was wide, flat,
and brown, with a lot of lawn.

McAlister had been driving for three hours, and the back
of his neck was stiff. He put on his tie and his suitcoat and
took the gun from the seat where it had been hidden under

the coat. Tucking it into his belt, he buttoned the suitcoat over it.

Having traveled the long flagstone walk to the front door, it was half a minute before anyone answered the bell. "Hello," she said. "Who do you want?"

She was a little girl carrying an open book.

"Evening," McAlister said. "Is Mr. Borland home?"

"Come on in," she said, stepping back.

"I'm sorry if I interrupted your reading."

"That's okay," she said. "Daddy's out back fixing the lawn mower. You sit down and I'll get him." She turned and walked away, holding the book up in front of her face.

McAlister stepped into the house and closed the door.

A woman called, "Who is it, dear?"

"It's a man for Daddy," the child said, walking down the hall toward the back of the house. The woman stepped into the hall, and the child swung left to avoid a collision.

The woman wore an apron and glasses. Her hair, as yellow as the child's, was tied in a knot at the back of her head. She had wide hips.

"How do you do," she said, holding out her hand. "I'm Alice Borland."

"McAlister," he said, "James McAlister. I hope I didn't catch you at a bad time. I'm an old friend of Sid's, and I was in the area so I thought I'd drop by."

"No, of course not," she said. There was something vague about her manner. Perhaps she was thinking about other things.

"I probably should have called," McAlister said. "Sid and I were in Korea together."

"Yes, in Korea." She said it as if friends from Korea and other places often dropped in. "Why don't we go into the living room? Sid should be in in a minute." He followed her into the living room.

Photographs of children covered the wall over the sofa. McAlister recognized the little girl with the braids. One boy looked particularly like his mother. He said, "These are your children?"

"Yes," she said, "a friend of ours is a photographer. He took most of them last summer. We liked them so much we had them framed."

"They're very nice," McAlister said.

"Can I get you a drink?"

"That's all right."

"Well," she said, "won't you sit down?"

He sat. "It's been a long while," he said. "When I knew Sid, he was a bachelor. Things have changed."

She laughed. "They certainly have. We have six children."

"That was the youngest one I saw?"

"No, there are two younger. Fortunately, this is the television hour or they'd be running through here like wild Indians." She pushed her glasses up on her thin nose. "You were with Sidney in Korea?"

"Yes," he said. "We were in prison together."

"In China?" She looked at him. "Oh," she said, "Sidney has told me about it. He'll be delighted to see you."

"We were on the plane together."

They heard the kitchen door slam. "There's Sidney now," she said.

Borland stopped for a second when he saw McAlister, but the hesitation was as between strangers, not long-lost friends. He had gotten heavy and bald. McAlister realized that he might have walked right past him on the street without recognizing him. And the way Borland was acting showed that twenty years had wrought an effective disguise for McAlister, too.

He nodded cautiously at McAlister. "Hello," he said, "how are you?"

He wiped the grease from his hands onto his dingy gray sweatshirt. "Lawn mower won't start," he said. "But I'm darned if I'm going to buy a new one."

"Darling," his wife said, "do you know who this is?"

His eyes moved up and down over McAlister.

"James McAlister," she said brightly, "from Korea. You were in prison together."

"Well, I'll be a son-of-a-bitch," he said. "I'll be a green-eyed son-of-a-bitch." He wiped his right hand once more on his shirt and then presented it to McAlister. "Where the hell did you come from?"

"Hello, Sid," McAlister said, shaking his hand. "How are you?"

"I thought you were still over there." He glanced from McAlister to his wife. "But you look good. You're in good shape. Son-of-a-bitch," he said. "You know, Alice, we were in prison together over there, eight, nine months. They must have the worst prisons in the world, Alice. Awful. I told you about it. One of the guys died, Lee, old Captain Lee, just because they gave him such lousy care. That's right, isn't it,

McAlister? Son-of-a-bitch, but it's good to see you. How about a drink?"

"I offered him a drink, but I wasn't able to persuade him to accept."

"Sure he'll have a drink," Borland said. "Won't you, old buddy?" He made a fist and tapped McAlister on the arm. "Anyway, when did you get back?"

"Just a little while ago. You're looking well, Sid."

"Oh, yeah, I'm fine. Let's see, it's been so damn long. I've got six kids. You met one of them."

"The little girl with the book," McAlister said.

"She reads all the time," Mrs. Borland said. "While you two talk, I've got to get back to the kitchen. I've got supper on the stove."

"That's all right, hon," Borland said. "I'll fix drinks. You go ahead."

She pushed her glasses up once more on her thin nose, smiled vaguely and left the room.

Borland grunted. He walked to the window and looked out. For a second he didn't say anything. The television set was playing loud off somewhere inside the house.

"What do you want to drink?" Borland said, without turning around. His tone had changed abruptly with his wife's departure.

"A little rye on the rocks, if you have it. This is a nice place, Sid. Comfortable."

"I do okay," he said, turning, his hands shoved in his baggy pockets. "I didn't see anything in the newspapers about them letting you out. Why are you here?"

"They let me come back. I thought I'd visit an old friend. I've got some questions I'm trying to answer, and I thought you might be able to help me."

"Yeah, sure," Borland said. His hands still in his pockets, he walked across the room toward a cabinet built into the bookshelf on the far wall. The sweatshirt and khaki pants hung loosely on his big frame.

He pulled open one of the cabinet doors. "I expected you," he said, "but not so soon."

"*Expected* me?"

He turned to look at McAlister with one hand still on the handle of the cabinet door. "Yeah," he said, "that's right. I expected you. A guy from the F.B.I. came by. He thought you might have been here already, and he said I should expect you. They want to talk to you."

"The F.B.I.?"

"I can tell a spook any place, and he wasn't one. Do you want that rye on the rocks?" He reached up to take a bottle out of the cabinet.

"Yes," McAlister said, "on the rocks." They had been looking for him. They knew he was here. What about Felix Klass?

Borland put ice in the glasses. "He was an F.B.I. man all right. He showed me his identification. I'm supposed to call him if you get in touch with me."

"Did he say why?"

"They're a little worried about you, and they want to talk to you. He said you came back on your own. I guess it bothers them."

Borland came across the room holding out the glass. His eyes moved nervously from McAlister, to the window, to the drink.

"Thanks," McAlister said. He took a sip. "Did he say what they want to talk to me about?"

Borland walked back to the cabinet. "You didn't think they were looking for you?"

"No, I didn't. But Felix Klass said I should talk to you."

"Who?"

"Felix Klass. He talked to you maybe a week ago."

"Never heard of him." He fixed his own drink with his back to McAlister. "You and Roberts," he said, "you got a raw deal. They didn't have to leave you over there."

"That's right," McAlister said.

"Did you come back alone?"

"Roberts is still there. We're both under what you might call house arrest."

"Except they let you come back to the States."

"Only for a visit," McAlister said. "I want to get some things straightened out."

"Like what?" He turned. The liquor swung around in his glass.

"We could start off with Klass."

"I told you I never heard of him."

"Maybe you've seen him." He took out the folded picture of Felix Klass and opened it. It was the picture the General had given him. The crease ran just below Klass's moon face, right across his bow tie. He held it out.

"Why sure," Borland said, looking at the photograph and

then at McAlister. "That's George Frost. He took those pictures of the kids." He gestured toward the wall over the sofa. "He's a neighbor—lives down the street."

"He also calls himself Felix Klass."

"I never heard him called that. What do you want him for?"

"I think he can help me with some information."

Borland smiled and handed back the picture. "Not right now," he said. "They're away. Europe. Alice will know. She's very friendly with his wife, and I think she said they were going for the whole summer. They only left a couple of days ago."

"How long has he been living here."

"A couple of years. They travel a lot. He's a hell of a good photographer, but he's in some kind of import-export business. What information do you need?"

"A lot," McAlister said. "Sid, I want to find out who sabotaged the plane."

"Christ, that was years ago."

"You got out. And you were going to get us out."

Borland shook his head. "They all said we were wrong, Jim. The Chinese must have shot it down. An explosive shell could have blown out the side."

"That's crap and you know it."

"I told you guys I'd do my best. And I did. I did everything I could." His face was flushed. In the dim light, the smear of grease on his cheek looked like a slash.

"You could have gone to the newspapers."

Borland took his glass to the bar and poured a refill. "I did what I could," he said.

"You didn't do anything." Mrs. Borland was coming down the hall. McAlister continued. "I want to know why you didn't even try."

She stepped into the room. "Didn't try what?" she asked, smiling.

"We were talking about prison," Borland said quickly.

"Oh," she said. She pushed her glasses up on her nose and looked at McAlister. "If you don't mind the children," she said, "we'd love to have you stay for dinner."

"McAlister has children," Borland said.

"Thanks, but I can't."

"We have plenty of food, Mr. McAlister, and we'd enjoy having you. Maybe you'll change your mind." She turned to go.

McAlister waited until she had gone back down the hall. "What happened when you got back, Sid? Did they buy you off?"

Borland wiped his hand across his gray sweatshirt again. "You don't have to talk like that."

"We expected too much, Sid. We shouldn't have trusted you."

"I didn't ask to do it. You guys pushed it on me."

"I know. And you didn't ask to go down in the plane, and you didn't ask for anything else either."

"Why don't you go?"

"Because I still have to get some answers."

"Not from me."

"Tell me about the plane, and Klass or George Frost."

"I told you all I know about Frost." He looked at McAlister. "Wait a minute. We had talked about you. He read a magazine article, and started asking me questions. But that was a year ago."

"What did you tell him?"

"What happened, the facts."

"About the explosives?"

"Well, no," Borland said, shaking his drink. "He wasn't very interested in that. He just wanted to know what happened to everyone who was on the plane."

"Did you tell him why you didn't get us out?"

"No, I didn't," Borland said. "I didn't have any choice, McAlister. The Air Force and the Agency told me it was none of my business."

"You were supposed to raise hell."

"I was still in uniform and under orders."

"You got out of the service."

"It wasn't that simple." He took a few steps across the darkening room, walking heavily in his baggy pants. "They had it all worked out," he said, "right from the beginning, right from Hong Kong.

"They treated me like a traitor. As soon as the doctor checked me, they flew me to Japan for debriefing. I was under guard all the time. They kept asking why I signed the statement, and they wouldn't believe we had agreed on it. They wouldn't believe anything."

He walked to the black window and looked out. "They were most angry about the part of the statement that said the plane was sabotaged, time-bombed to go down inside China. That drove them out of their minds. They wouldn't listen to anything, and they told me what to say."

"You didn't have to."

"What do you mean I didn't have to? I was still in uniform. One of the generals, Timmers or Thompson, put it on the line. Obey orders or take a court martial for aiding the enemy and that could be twenty years in jail."

"They'd already given *us* forty years."

"The Agency people said they would do everything they could to get you out. So I gave the right answers. You know, yes, we were off course; yes, you and Roberts were civilian employees of the Defense Department."

"When you got back to the States you could have done something."

"It was worse. I went down to the Agency, but they said they didn't have anybody to exchange, and they couldn't ransom you out."

"And you gave up."

"For a while I kept poking around. I talked to the crew chief, Ralph Peters, you remember him?"

"What did he say?"

"I think he was lying."

"And you didn't do anything about it."

"Will you cut it out. I'm trying to help you."

"All right. What did Peters say?"

"He was still in the Air Force, and he got so upset I had to give him a few weeks to cool off. I was going to go back and get the truth out of him."

"But you didn't."

"That's right. I didn't. I couldn't. I was married, and I had to make a living. I went to work for the airline, and they sent me out to Denver for training maybe a month after I talked to Peters. I was out there only a few days, when I got a call. A guy from the F.B.I. visited me. He said they thought maybe the Communists would try to use me.

"They had a report I had bothered Peters. The F.B.I. said they expected me to leave problems of foreign affairs to the State Department and the C.I.A. In other words, I should keep my mouth shut. And I had my job and my family at stake."

Mrs. Borland called the children for dinner. As they paraded through, they looked at their father with hopeful eyes. He waved them on. "I'll be in soon," he promised. Each of them studied McAlister a little, and then they went down the hallway. They were nice looking kids.

It wasn't Sid Borland's fault. Borland was just like everybody else. It was their own fault. They had expected too much.

"Another drink?" Borland asked.

"No thanks. What about Peters?"

"He was scared. I think he knew who did it, but he had been told to keep his mouth shut."

"Where can I find him?"

"I don't know." He shrugged. "He was out in California for a while. Then, a couple of years ago, I heard he was living on Long Island, working for Grumman."

"Did you tell any of this to Klass, George Frost?"

He looked at McAlister. "You know that's right. It was Frost who told me about Peters. He had seen him somewhere on the Island."

"Had he talked to him?"

"I don't know. What does George Frost have to do with this?"

"I'm not sure," McAlister said. "Maybe Peters will know."

"You're going to talk to Peters?"

"If I can find him."

"What difference does it make now?"

"Let's call it curiosity."

"You don't want me to tell the F.B.I.?"

"I want a couple of days."

"They could always find a way to lift my commercial license."

"All I can do is ask, Sid. I'm asking you to take a small chance. Maybe you'll want to even things up a little."

Borland stared at him. "Why don't you go to the Bureau first?"

"I want to do it this way. A few days, Sid."

"You'll keep me out of it?"

"Two days." McAlister was walking toward the front door.

"I'll do my best," Borland said.

"Just don't do anything," McAlister said, stopping. "That way I won't have to come back."

"What do you mean by that?"

"What do you think I mean, Sid? Because of you, we spent three years rotting in that prison. I'd rather we just forget each other, because if I come back here it won't be friendly."

Borland shoved his fist into the pockets of his baggy pants. "I don't like people threatening me."

"Take care of yourself," McAlister said as he pulled the door open and stepped outside.

Borland watched him go into the darkness. He could see the car parked on the road. If he went out after him, he could get the license number of the car. But McAlister would know what he was doing. He shoved the door closed and headed for the bar. "Son-of-a-bitch," he said under his breath.

McAlister is trying to prove something, but it was too long ago. What difference does it make now? He has been over there for a long while. He might be working for them. And why is he looking for George Frost? He should tell the F.B.I. about Frost, too.

He drank half the whiskey.

He thought, son-of-a-bitch, coming in here like I owe him something. All right. Years in that prison where the stones were always cold and you froze to death every day, even in the spring. The worst part was that you couldn't talk to anyone unless you wanted to talk to their propaganda people. A few months had been murder. McAlister had three years. He must have gone out of his mind.

He finished the drink.

Captain Lee and I weren't spooks, he thought. We were Air Force. That's why they let me out. Maybe if McAlister and Roberts had signed a statement, too, in the early days, they would have let them out after the trial.

He poured another drink.

"Sidney," his wife said, "Sidney, aren't you coming in to dinner?"

"Put something aside for me, will you, Alice? I'll eat something later." He was standing with his hands on the edge of the cabinet. She could see he had a lot on his mind—old friends bring old memories, she thought, as she left quietly.

Clutching his glass of warm whiskey, he made his way into the library, stopping first to look out the window beside the front door. Putting his face close to the pane, he could see the car was gone.

He walked deliberately toward the photographs hanging above his desk. Most of them were in black frames. One of them showed the crew lined up in front of the Skymaster: Captain Harold Lee and Lieutenant Sidney A. Borland, both wearing leather jackets, and then the two sergeants, Joe Boyle and Wylie, who took care of cargo, and Master Sergeant Ralph J. Peters, crew chief, grinning on the end. The picture could have been taken yesterday.

There wasn't any picture of the spooks, Roberts and McAlister, and the Chinese, because they had just been passengers.

There were other photographs, too, taken at Andrews just before he got his commission. He had been a skinny kid. There was a picture of him when he had joined the ferry wing, and then that crazy snapshot with the six little Japanese girls all dressed up in kimonos surrounding him like a bunch of butterflies while he grinned.

And there was the newspaper article about his release. Alice had saved and framed it for him. "Chinese Release U.S. Hero Flyer."

Hero U.S. flyer, shit. He drank half the whiskey and put the glass on the desk.

He had seniority now. He was third senior pilot of the division, and he had the run he wanted. He went out for a couple of days straight and then he had time off.

"Son-of-a-bitch," he said softly.

He got up and shut the door and then sat down at his desk. For a long while he sat with his elbows on the desk, his face in his hands. His belly was pushing against the drawer.

He heard the children come into the television room and turn on the set. Flying was all he knew. He couldn't make a living at anything else. They were still paying off the mortgage, and the children had to go to college. He was saving only a hundred dollars a month, twelve hundred a year. There wasn't more than six or seven thousand in the bank, and even her old man hadn't left very much despite all his talk, maybe fifteen thousand in stock, which was no fortune.

The television set was blaring. He went to the door, yanked it open. "Turn that thing down," he yelled.

His voice was thick. The children stared at him. He had poured down a lot of liquor. He slammed the door.

He went back to the desk and shoved the chair aside. I must not sound tight now, he thought, or they'll think I'm some drunk.

He picked up the telephone on the desk and dialed Operator.

"Operator," he said, "I want to get the F.B.I., the Federal Bureau of Investigation, in New York City."

Chapter

16

McALISTER had parked on the south side of the street. In the darkness all the houses had looked alike, but with dawn the differences began to appear.

The house across the street had a breezeway and an extension on the garage. A white car was parked in the driveway. According to the telephone directory and the number on the house beside it, this was the home of Ralph J. Peters, the only Ralph Peters listed in Suffolk County.

The sky was gray. There were lights in a few of the houses on the street, and now a light went on downstairs deep inside Peters' house. McAlister turned a little in his seat to more carefully watch the door and the breezeway.

A man entered the breezeway, putting on a leather jacket as he walked. He had a piece of toast in his mouth. Jumping down onto the lawn, he stopped to zip up his jacket. The last of the toast disappeared into his mouth.

He was a little, plump man with a thick head of brown hair. As he yanked open the door of the dirty white car, he looked back down the driveway into the street. He was staring at McAlister. A man waiting in a parked car couldn't be a common sight in the suburbs, and the early hour must have made it even more odd. But Peters was not dismayed. He slid into his car, pulling the door closed behind him.

McAlister got out and crossed the asphalt road. Peters had started his car. It was pumping out white smoke, and it started coming backward down the gravel driveway. As it came by, McAlister yelled Peters' name and waved one hand.

The car stopped short. A window rolled down. "You shouldn't be here," he said, whispering furiously. "I told you guys not to come out here."

"I want to talk to you for a few minutes."

"Get in the car." His voice was tense. "Get in the car."

Peters had taken him for someone else, but next to Peters was where he wanted to be, so McAlister opened the door and got in.

"Leave the door alone. I'll shut it." Peters growled. He leaned across and held the door handle down, closing the door silently. Then he continued backing down the drive.

"I thought it was one of you guys across the street," he said. "I told you not to come out here."

Clear of the driveway, he jammed the gear handle into drive and went ahead slowly.

"You wake me up in the middle of the night, even

though I told you you could talk to me out at the plant or when I get off. You didn't have to come to the house."

McAlister grunted, wondering how long it would take Peters to realize he had the wrong man. He said, "What harm does it do?"

"I told you last night my wife's been sick. She's been getting crazy ideas. If she sees the F.B.I. hanging around the house, she's apt to go crackers."

"I'm sorry."

Peters pulled a package of cigarettes out of the pocket of his jacket. He shook the pack so the cigarettes came up, offered one to McAlister and put one in his mouth. Then he pushed in the dashboard lighter.

"She's had kidney trouble for years," he said. The unlit cigarette bobbed up and down as he spoke. "For a while she believed she was getting poisoned. The doctor's giving her pills, and he says she'll get over it. But I have to keep her from getting excited."

The lighter popped out. He lit the cigarette, puffed hard. "So what happens? The telephone rings in the middle of the night. She answers and you guys say it's the F.B.I. calling for me."

He swung the cigarette through the air. "Then I spend half the night trying to convince her it's just a routine check you're making at the plant. If she happened to wake up and see you at the house, what was she going to think?"

McAlister shut his eyes for a second and leaned back on the seat. He said, "I just want to talk to you for a few minutes." He had been lucky. Borland must have called the Bureau the minute he had left.

"What the hell do you have to talk to me about?" Peters was driving faster now. "I told you I'd let you know if that guy contacts me."

"You mean McAlister?"

"Yeah. Him or the other one."

"Roberts?"

"Even if they let them out, they wouldn't have any reason to see me." He puffed on the cigarette, slowed and turned onto the highway, a four-lane road with a grass divider in the center. Peters picked up speed, going faster than the traffic, traveling west with the orange sky behind them. In the cool morning the countryside was flat and gray with mist.

"Peters," McAlister said. "We know each other."

"What do you mean by that?"

"I think we've met before."

Peters stared at him. "You don't look familiar," he said. "I don't know any people in the F.B.I."

They were catching up to an old brown Volkswagen. Peters honked twice and swung out to go around it. Four large men were packed inside. The driver was smoking a cigar. He waved his hand as they went by.

"Friends of mine," Peters said. "We work in the same shop."

They sped through an intersection and then Peters said, "Okay, let's have it. What's the information that's so important you had to come out to the house?" He finished the cigarette and flicked it out through the open crack at the top of the window.

They were passing one car after another, and the car

seemed to shake a little. At this rate it would not take long to get to the plant.

"You may not know me, but I recognize you. I'm James McAlister."

The round face turned toward him, the eyes wide.

"I'm McAlister. Borland said I should talk to you."

"I thought you were . . ."

"I'm surprised you didn't recognize me."

Peters swung the car to the right and slowed. "What the hell are you bothering me for? You've got no business bothering me."

"Borland said you could tell me something about the crash."

"The F.B.I. said you're helping the Communists. Why should I tell you anything?" He was stopping the car at the side of the road.

"I'm not helping anybody," McAlister said. "Borland said you had some idea who sabotaged the plane."

"You were on it. You know what happened. All I know is what I was told. It was shot down."

"You know better than that."

"I was in the Air Force. I just took care of it."

"You didn't take very good care of it."

"I don't want to talk to you. Just get the hell out."

He stopped the car. The Volkswagen went by, horn blaring.

"Let's keep driving," McAlister said. "I've got some questions I want to ask you."

"Yeah, sure. So does the F.B.I." Peters was looking

straight ahead with both hands still holding the wheel. "I'm not going to help you, McAlister. I'm not going to tell you anything. I've got enough troubles of my own."

"It would make it easier for both of us if you'd give me a few facts. Borland said you know who put the charges on the plane."

"I never really believed that story about explosives. Now are you going to get out here? Write me a letter or something."

"Take it easy," McAlister said.

"I don't have to talk to you. Now get out or I'll throw you out."

"Listen to me," McAlister said softly. "Captain Lee was killed, and they sentenced Roberts and me. We spent years in prison. I'm not here to play games, Peters."

"Yeah. How long do you want to sit here? Maybe the F.B.I. is waiting for me at the plant. They'll wonder where I am. Maybe they'll come looking for me."

McAlister touched the .32 and took it out. It was heavy in his hand, resting on his thigh. "Now," he said, "let's drive a little."

Peters glanced at him and at the gun. "Put that thing away," he said quietly, a tremor breaking in his voice.

"Let's drive." McAlister gestured with the gun.

"All right. All right." Peters stepped on the accelerator and pulled out onto the highway.

"We'll turn around," McAlister said. "We'll go back to your house."

"My house? What about my wife? If she sees you waving that thing around, after the F.B.I., she's liable to crack."

"That's your problem. Take the turnaround up ahead," McAlister said, lifting the gun slightly.

Peters flicked his turn indicator and slowed. "She doesn't have anything to do with this, and she's not well. This could scare hell out of her. Like I told you, the doctor says she's a little paranoid, and . . ."

"Just make the turn," McAlister said.

He pulled into the turnaround and stopped. "If I talk to you, what happens?"

"It will be a secret between you and me. Then I disappear. You'll never see me again. We won't get near your place."

"And the F.B.I.?" Peters drove onto the highway.

"You do whatever you want. Call them up. Tell them I tried to get you to talk and then I left."

"You don't care?"

"Not now. All I want is some information."

Peters glanced at McAlister. "Let me tell you something, McAlister," he said, "when the time comes, I'll get you. If I ever see you again anywhere around my place, I'll get you. I mean it."

McAlister's right knee was shaking a little. He reached down and rubbed it. "Who did it, Peters?" he said. "And why?"

"Okay," Peters said. He had two hands on the wheel. "It was raining hard that night, you remember, one of those Korean rains. You couldn't see a hundred feet. It stopped just before you guys took off."

"I remember."

"The DC–6, the Castle, had only a couple of hundred

hours when we got it. It was in good shape and I took care of my airplanes.

"I remember the orders. She was supposed to be made ready for maximum range. Someone had added that we should top the tanks all the way. We got the fuel truck.

"As soon as the truck finished, we gave the plane a running check. We went right down the list on each engine, and everything checked. Then we had an hour or more before the captain was coming out, and the rain was still coming down."

He puffed again on his cigarette. "It was a couple of hundred yards to the coffee shack by the hangars, and we both wanted coffee. I remember we thought of asking the tower to send a jeep, but then the rain let up a little, and we figured it would be quicker to make a run for it."

Someone honked behind them. Peters turned slowly off the highway onto an asphalt road that wandered between development homes, painted gray with white trim. "We can drive around for a few minutes, and then I'll take you back to your car."

"Then what happened?" McAlister had waited twenty years for this story.

"We had coffee in the shack," Peters continued. "The rain kept coming down hard. We were just finishing when I looked out at the plane. A jeep was out there.

"I should have gone out there in the rain and checked it, but I figured it was Captain Lee or Borland. When Lee was flying for the sneaky petes, I mean for you guys, he was always a nut about things, and he made his own check.

"A couple of seconds later the jeep comes past the shack.

It was your jeep, you know, with the busted windshield."

"Who was driving?"

"It was raining like hell and I couldn't make him out, and I really didn't care then. It didn't make any difference.

"After it stopped raining and you guys took off, I found the jeep near the fuel tanks. It wasn't supposed to be parked there, so I drove it over to the motor pool. I parked it, and I was getting out when I saw something yellow under the seat. I pulled it, and what comes out but a wet plastic wrapper with black letters stenciled on it. It was a dynamite wrapper and there were still some caps in it. At the time it didn't mean anything more than that someone had used the jeep to haul dynamite. The cover was wet so they had used it during the rain.

"In the morning I heard that you guys didn't make it back. The reports said it was probably ground fire. They got you with a lucky hit."

"Pull over here and park," McAlister said.

"Jeez," Peters said. "I shouldn't be telling you this." But he parked the car where McAlister indicated.

Ahead of them on the sidewalk two boys in sweaters were carrying their books in knapsacks. They called to another boy in a blue jacket who was waiting on the lawn farther down the block.

McAlister took out his wallet and found the folded picture of Felix Klass. He handed it to Peters. "Have you ever seen this fellow? He calls himself George Frost."

Peters studied the picture and shook his head slowly. "I don't think so," he said. "But I don't have a good memory for faces. Was he over there?"

"No," McAlister said, taking the picture. "You would have seen him here, in the last few years."

"He doesn't look familiar."

"All right," McAlister said, taking back the picture and putting it away. "Who drove that jeep?"

"I never really found out," Peters said. He turned on the ignition. He was sweating.

"Now wait a minute," McAlister said. "You must have had some idea."

Peters looked at him, and then at the gun and back at McAlister's face. He turned off the ignition.

"If you ever tell anybody I'll deny it," he said. "I'll swear I never talked to you, you hear me?"

"Who was it?"

"I talked to the fuel truck monkey. He said he saw the guy get out of the jeep. It was the right jeep because it had the busted windshield, but he didn't recognize the guy.

"I took him over to that office at the south end. We parked and watched the spooks leave that night, and he spotted the guy."

"All right. Who was it?"

Peters looked straight ahead into the morning sunlight. He had both hands on the wheel. "It was the big guy. I think he was running the job you guys were on, but he had only been out to the DC, the Castle, a couple of times, Cunningham."

McAlister stared at him for a second. Peters' round eyes looked down at the gun and back out to the road. His face was moist with sweat. He dug out his cigarettes.

McAlister said, "Was it Cummings?"

"Yeah," he said. "Cunningham or Cummings, that was it."

He should have known it all these years because it was perfectly obvious, really. It was the only thing that made sense. Cummings.

Chapter

17

"COME in and sit down," Colonel Rynders said, glancing up from his desk. "I thought I was the only insomniac around here."

"It's not that early," Cummings said, glancing at his watch. It was a few minutes after eight o'clock in the morning. "I've got some information, but I'm not happy about it."

"The Chinaman?"

"We've identified him. It's McAlister."

The Colonel already knew what Cummings had come to tell him. "That's what I heard," he said.

"We're going to get him tomorrow, if we have any luck."

"That's good work," the Colonel said, pushing up his glasses so he could see better. Cummings looked like a big black bird, one hand on the back of the leather chair like an outspread wing.

They would have to go slow now, but convincing Cummings and D.I.A. was going to be a problem.

He said, "Just let me finish signing these letters."

"No hurry," Cummings said, sitting down in the chair.

Colonel Rynders was taking letters and memos from a stack on his left. He put each letter in the center of the desk, glanced through it, signed it and placed it on another pile at his right.

Two hours ago, he had made his morning check with the Bureau. They had told him the Chinaman was McAlister. They had suspected he was back in the States, and he was. Cummings' information confirmed his identity. It fit, but you still couldn't be sure he was the man they had dropped.

He had checked McAlister's file and dug out the letters and the Agency's debriefing. The record showed only what he already knew. McAlister had built a new life there. He had a wife, children, and apparently was a successful engineer.

The Agency once had tried to set up a contact. But it had failed, and that was ten years ago. There wasn't much from the last few years except copies of letters to McAlister from old friends, and the answers—none conveying anything except the memories of a half-forgotten relationship.

Twenty years is a long time, long enough for almost any kind of change, even loyalties. It had always been possible that McAlister was their agent, even a wet agent. But Colonel Rynders didn't worry about possibilities, because you could list them, evaluate them, and put your finger on each good one and check it out. It was the ones you didn't see that caused the problems. And there was something wrong with all the possibilities they had on the Chinaman. It scared him.

He signed another letter. Cummings had closed his eyes. Usually he looked like he had spent the last week on the tennis court, but this morning he looked exhausted.

The Colonel was worried. How could he persuade them to proceed slowly? There was too much they did not know, and that meant danger. Moving fast could be just what the Russians or the Chinese wanted.

"The rest can wait," he said, tossing the letter on the pile. He took off his thick glasses and put them on the desk. He felt like rubbing his eye, but instead he pinched the bridge of his nose. He could feel his eye roll a little.

"I talked with the Bureau this morning," he said. "I told them to get on him as fast as they can, but no arrest. I want him tracked, no matter how many men they need."

"That's what I want to talk to you about. We've got to pick him up if we can."

"It's too soon," the Colonel said.

"He called Martha," Cummings said.

"On the telephone? He identified himself?"

"That's right, but he wanted her to keep it a secret."

"Damn foolishness," Rynders said. He folded and unfolded his glasses on the desk. "He wants to get picked up."

"I'm not so sure," Cummings said. "He wanted Martha to set up a meeting with you."

"When?"

"He told her he would call back, but I don't think he's

going to. It was a cover. He could have called you directly just as easily."

"He's dropping leads, Gene. What did he tell her?"

"A two-minute telephone call. Before she really realized who it was, he had hung up. He asked her to set up a meeting with you, and then he said he would call back. I've had the telephone company and the Bureau on it in case he does call, but so far he hasn't."

"He knows better than that."

"You still think he's here to disrupt the talks?"

"He could be a sacrifice. He may not even know it. They may have something worked out, waiting for us. The Bureau said he contacted this fellow Borland."

"Borland's clean. We had him in the net because he was in prison with McAlister and Roberts. He was the copilot that they let out. We're pulling everyone off Roberts and putting them on McAlister. General Whooten wants him picked up right away."

"What did McAlister want from Borland?"

"He asked about our crew chief, a fellow named Peters. We're on him, too."

"They're trying to sandbag us."

"You're not worried about an assassination?"

"It's a possibility," Rynders said. But there were others to be considered as well. "If it's the KGB or the Army, and if they want to disrupt the talks and discredit Menshikov, they've got to be careful. It has to appear that we're the cause of the disruption, not them."

"If we had picked him up on the drop and made allegations, we would have created the incident. They could deny

185

the whole thing. Their reason for using McAlister has to be that he's ours. Their story would be believed, especially by Menshikov.

"They must have gone to a hell of a lot of trouble to recruit him. Any charges, any reports, anything that leaks out will only make us look absurd.

"But an assassination could backfire, especially an attempt during the talks. It has to be more subtle than that. They want to sandbag us.

"As soon as the Bureau locates him, we'll track him. We aren't going to pick him up until we have a good idea why they want us to get him."

"D.I.A. won't buy it."

"That's their problem."

"Harry Rivers is coming over."

"When?"

"Soon," Cummings said. "Harry's going to make sure we pick him up as soon as possible. They want the Agency out of it."

"What did you tell him?"

"General Whooten called me. I told him it was up to you. But Whooten said we shouldn't be making the decisions because he was one of our people."

"They want to stick with their wet agent theory. But this is Agency responsibility, and that's the way the Director wants it and that's the way the President wants it."

"That's what I thought you'd say. But they're not going to like it, Colonel," Cummings said. "They'll fight you."

"I know," Colonel Rynders said. "Why don't you get

Harry down here now and bring the file on McAlister, too. I'd like to look at it again. And let's bring Sievert in on it. If we've got a tracking operation, he may have some people we can lend the Bureau. It could take a lot of manpower."

Rynder's head was aching, and he rubbed the back of his neck. "I'll wait for you," he said, as he reached down and pulled open his right desk drawer where he kept the aspirin. The door closed behind Cummings.

Colonel Rynders put the bottle on his desk. It was half empty. He poured three aspirins into his palm, tossed them gently into his mouth, and chewed. They tasted bitter.

Townsend and Whooten figured they had something now, and they were moving in, despite the risk. If picking up McAlister meant they'd be walking into something that could blow up the talks, they wouldn't mind because they were against the talks anyway. And they could blame the Agency.

He put the cap back on the bottle and tucked it in the drawer. It always took a while before the aspirin worked. Then the pain would diminish, but he would still feel its full force lurking.

They had built Defense Intelligence, and they had been moving in for years, trying to take over all military intelligence and counter-intelligence, foreign and domestic. General Townsend had actually put it in writing, a formal proposal urging a separate but equal agency. One thing like this which impacted the talks, and General Townsend was close enough to the President to swing it. There wasn't anybody now who would stand up against the generals except the

Agency, not even State. When the President isn't politically tied to disarmament (and this one wasn't), they would be able to prove anything they wanted.

This would be the first step, and then, maybe in five or ten or fifteen years, when they had a big problem, the generals would have all the answers, all the intelligence foreign and domestic. And with the Pentagon and D.I.A. proving they were right, they would control the entire country.

There was a single knock, and the door opened. It was the Colonel's secretary, Katie Neilson. She always came in first thing to see if he wanted coffee. She was twenty-three or -four, attractive and professional.

"Good morning," she said. "Can I get you some coffee?"

"It's always a pleasure to see you in the morning," Colonel Rynders said and he meant it. She seemed to lighten his burden somehow. "I could use a black coffee."

Katie waited for a moment while he signed some letters. Sometimes he asked for a bottle of aspirin too. He was tired. Katie could tell by his scar which curved like a faint new moon above his cheekbone. Sometimes in the morning it was hardly visible, but when he was tired and had one of his headaches the scar was so bright she could see it from across the office.

He was still reading the letter. "Katie," he said, without looking up, "I understand I have a nickname."

"What?" she said, surprised. She had expected his request for aspirins.

He glanced up over the glasses. "A nickname. I have a nickname. I wonder if you have heard it?"

She felt herself blush, because everyone knew the nickname. It made sense with his thick glasses, but he wasn't really a cold fish like the name implied.

"No," she lied.

"You mean you never heard a nickname for me?"

"If it was a nice nickname I'd tell you," she said, smiling. "And if it wasn't, I wouldn't."

"How about 'Fish'?" he said. "Is that a nice nickname?"

"I think it's awful," she said.

When he smiled he looked like a boy. "Well, it's probably better than no nickname."

"It's because of the glasses."

"I hope so," he said, and signed the letter. "That's the last one. You want to take them?"

"Yes, sir," she said. "Would you like anything with the coffee?"

"Just black," he said, "and you better get me some aspirin."

"A bottle?"

"I don't want to run out," he said.

"I'll be right back." As she left, her hair caught the light like water. A glimpse of the brightly lit corridor and someone going by flashed into view before the door swung shut.

Colonel Rynders sat back, thinking that maybe it was this damn McAlister business that kept the headache beating strong. It should have started going by now. Something worried him and he couldn't put his finger on the particular fact. These situations were like that, you couldn't explain it, but if you were close enough, you could feel it building wrong.

It had happened before. There had been awkward pieces and things didn't fit. Like the light. It should have flashed quickly, but instead it made two long flashes. Then, sitting in the rowboat, peering into the darkness, he had sensed something was wrong. But he had been a damn fool. He had moved too fast.

He had been working with the partisans just north of the Po, and after the light he had rowed on quietly to the shore of the lake, right into the hands of the Germans.

He had heard a movement behind him, and he had started to turn, expecting to hear the password. "Gettysburg," he said quietly.

When he woke later he was shaking all over and he had a bump like a rock on his head and blood matted in his hair. They had beaten him, stripped him, and left him for dead.

He had woken all in pain, struggling up out of a tunnel of darkness. He couldn't see out of either eye, and his head ached. He did not understand why the partisans spent so much time bandaging his left eye. The camp doctor told him why later. The eyeball had been hanging out.

Despite the beating, he had brought them together, and when they got the radio going he had called in supplies. He had done a good job. And while he lay on the ground in that smoky cave, suffering, they had raised hell. They got him out a month later—too late to save his eye. They had given him plastic, and he had never seen well again.

Luckily, the Office of Strategic Service had desk jobs at home. If he had still been in the Army they would have retired him from service. Blind men can't cut that kind of mustard. But he could work with the new C.I.A.

And he had done pretty well. In two reports he had been called one of the "fine guiding intelligences," and he had had good success in Guatemala. He was proud of the Agency, really. Not only because of what they'd accomplished, but because of what they'd prevented the generals from doing, especially in the last few years.

He closed his eyes, listening to the throbbing in his head. Then he pulled open the desk drawer again and shook two tablets out of the bottle of aspirins. Tossing them into his mouth, he chewed.

Cummings knocked once and then entered the Colonel's office with the file in his hand. Captain Harry Rivers was right behind him, looking as tall and neat in his blue tailored suit as he might look in uniform.

"Morning, Colonel," Rivers said, smiling. "We're making progress. It won't be long now."

"Charlie Sievert was out, Colonel," Cummings said. "He'll be back in a few minutes. I left word."

"Thank you," the Colonel said. "You've done pretty well, Harry. Do you want some coffee? Katie just went to get it."

"I've had my breakfast," Rivers said, waving his hand. "General Whooten wanted me to sit in with Gene to see if we can be of any immediate help."

"I was telling Gene we have to go slow now," the Colonel explained. "And I told the Bureau no arrest. I want him tracked for a while."

"That's taking a chance, Colonel. If we try to track him, we could lose him. Then suppose he kills somebody."

"He's not going to kill anybody."

"Yes, sir," Rivers said, nodding his head. "But we don't agree with that estimate."

"I understand General Whooten feels that Defense Intelligence should take full responsibility."

"Yes, sir," Rivers said. "He believes that would be more diplomatic for all of us. McAlister is still tied to the Agency."

"He's been over there for many years."

"Yes, sir," Harry Rivers said.

"We can't move fast, Harry. It has to be a careful operation. He's been dropping leads all over the place, and they just might want us to pick him up. They may be sandbagging us."

"Yes, sir," Harry Rivers said. "But we don't concur on that."

"I'm aware you don't."

The door swung open. "Oh, excuse me," she said.

"It's all right, Katie," the Colonel said.

She carried the little tray with the coffee on it past Cummings and Rivers and set it down on the desk.

"You sure you don't want any coffee?" the Colonel asked.

"I'm fine," Harry Rivers said.

Cummings was standing behind the chair with his arms folded.

Harry Rivers continued. "I understand your position, Colonel, but we want an immediate arrest. McAlister is a wet agent. If he carries out his assignment, the disarmament talks will come to a halt."

"They wouldn't send him for that. They've got better people."

"I'm just carrying out orders," Harry Rivers said. "General Whooten asked me to work with Gene. He wants him picked up as soon as possible." He leaned forward. "General Whooten said that if there was any problem I should ask you or Mr. Lucas to call General Townsend."

"Townsend? How is he involved?"

"I don't know for certain, sir," Rivers said, and then a faint smile crossed his face. "I understand he has discussed it with the President."

"Damn it," Rynders said. "Sit down, Harry. And Gene, put the file on the desk and sit down, too." He turned in his chair, picked up the telephone and pushed the button for Katie.

"Yes, sir," she said.

"Will you get me General Townsend, please, Katie? I'll wait."

"Yes, sir," she said. "Right away."

Still holding the telephone, Rynders looked at Harry Rivers. "What do you mean he talked with the President about McAlister?"

"Yes, sir. He was with General Whooten when he told me to come over here and work with Gene."

The Colonel heard voices on the telephone. It was Townsend's aide. He cut in. "This is Isaac Rynders," he said, "Plans Division at the Agency. Let me speak to him, please."

"Yes, sir," the aide said. "Just one minute, please."

It took less than a minute. "This is Townsend. Isaac, how are you?"

"I'm fine, General. Captain Rivers is here, and there seems to be some question about how we're going to handle this McAlister business. Do you know what I'm talking about?"

"I certainly do, Isaac. I discussed it with the President this morning. Things are moving fast. Considering all the possibilities, particularly this man's background, he and I both feel it would be better if you folks let us run him to the ground. The hard part's done. General Whooten tells me that now it is only a matter of hours."

"It's not that simple."

"I understand your position, Isaac. But I think Lucas outlined it most ably to the President. We all feel that it's wise —the safer side of valor—to move as fast as we can."

"We'll play right into their hands."

"I'm not sure you're correct. But they can't make much of it, Isaac, no matter how it is arranged. The Bureau or C.I.C. will put him in cold storage for a while, no statements, no media, nothing will get out. We can deal with the situation in a more sophisticated manner when the talks are over."

"We're taking a chance."

"Maybe so, Isaac, but we'd like to do it this way, and the President concurs. Unless, of course, you have some information to which we are not privy."

"Does Lucas know about this?"

"I talked with him again a few minutes ago. He's not happy about it, but I think it is the safest solution. The President wants D.I.A. to take over."

"All right," Rynders said.

"Nice to talk with you, Isaac. We should get together one of these days, perhaps with Whooten. We can try to smooth out some of the wrinkles, interagency problems."

"I'd like to," Rynders said.

"I told Harry that the President wants to know the minute they pick him up. He's still pretty worried about it."

"We'll be sure he's informed."

"Thank you, Ike," the General said. "Goodbye."

"Goodbye," Rynders said. He put the telephone down. Townsend had put the Agency right in the middle so that if the talks blew up, McAlister would be the cause.

He glanced at Gene Cummings, who was still standing with his arms folded. He had been close to D.I.A. ever since he helped them reorganize. He knew what was going on, and he had known it all along.

"All right, gentlemen," the Colonel said. "I guess that's it. You're supposed to pick him up as fast as you can, and never mind anything else." He looked at Rivers. "You may be right, Harry. I hope to God you are."

Harry Rivers stood up. Colonel Rynders said, "Gene, why don't you leave that file with me for a few minutes? Let me go through it again, and send down copies of the daily report. I'd like to see them."

"Right away," Cummings said.

The Colonel watched them leave the room. The door closed. He was right. D.I.A. was going to use the incident for everything they could, and no matter what happened, General Townsend was going to get what he wanted, an independent intelligence agency.

He sipped the coffee. The aspirin was working. He could still feel the headache, but it had lessened. He reached over, picked up the telephone and pressed the button for Katie.

"Yes, sir," she said.

"Katie, would you ask Charlie Sievert to come down and see me as soon as he can? I'm going to need his help. And then go upstairs and tell Gene Cummings I've changed my mind. I'd like those files he has—all the files on the McAlister business, including the old file on the crash, when he went down."

"McAlister?" She wanted to get it right.

"Yes," Rynders said. "He'll know who you mean. The Chinaman."

Chapter **18**

EVERY Saturday Mrs. Judith Payne McAlister wrote an airmail letter to her son, James, and then took a walk to the church.

She wrote the letter on both sides of two flimsy blue pages, folded them, tucked them into an airmail envelope, and addressed it to Mr. Albert Wong Wertheimer, Commerce and Merchants Bank, 21 Queen Street, Hong Kong. Next, she sealed it carefully and put on the stamps.

Taking the letter, she walked slowly to the front hall and put it in her purse, which she always left on the table. Then she went to the kitchen to fix a cottage cheese sandwich and a cup of very hot tea—her lunch.

Except for the letter and her walk, Saturday was Mrs. McAlister's quiet day. Wednesday and Thursday she cleaned, did the ironing, and sewed. On Friday afternoon her garden club met, and Friday evening she generally went out for dinner. Sunday was church, reading the newspaper, and getting ready for the week.

She had just finished her hot tea this Saturday, when the telephone rang. Mrs. McAlister was getting old, and she was constrained to walk slowly. It was a long way from the kitchen to the other side of the living room. She reached the phone on the sixth or seventh ring.

"Hello," she said. No answer.

"Hello," she said again. "Who's calling?" The telephone clicked and the line went dead. Whoever it was had hung up. Perhaps they had the wrong number.

She walked back to the kitchen and cleaned up. When the kitchen was spotless, the way she liked it, she took her spring tweed coat out of the front closet and picked up her purse.

She had been looking forward to her walk and her visit to the church. And although the radio had predicted rain, when she walked out of the front door and pulled it shut, she was greeted by a pleasant, sunny day, warm but with a little breeze—just perfect for a walk.

On her way she dropped the letter into the mailbox at Marvin Street and went on down the hill toward the village. Sometimes she wondered whether Albert Wong Wertheimer really did exist. Mr. Kurlov who had met her in Hong Kong on the last trip had arranged for her to write to Mr. Wertheimer at the bank. The bank forwarded the mail. It was through the bank, too, that Mrs. McAlister sent a little something to James every month. A gift or baked goods. It wasn't much, but the boys might enjoy it.

In his last letter James had written about how Tu-chan and the boys were studying English. The boys learned it in school, and Tu-chan had joined a special evening class given primarily for the professional people in the town who were associated with the chemical plant and the factory. Tu-chan had written a few lines of English in her own hand, "Dear Mother, how are you? We are looking ahead to the visit you will make to us."

The first time Mrs. McAlister had visited them she had been afraid that, because Tu-chan was an engineer she would be like all the Russian women working at men's jobs she had seen in pictures. But Tu-chan was slender, gentle, and very feminine with delicate hands and happy eyes. She was a delightful surprise. And the boys were adorable, fat and golden-skinned. They had their father's blue eyes and their mother's black hair.

She was looking forward to her visit this year. Now that they could speak some English maybe she could get to know her grandsons and Tu-chan better. And, if everything worked out, maybe she could stay more than two weeks.

But Mrs. McAlister's most precious dream was that they would let James come home. He would bring Tu-chan and the boys, and the whole family would stay with her while they got used to American life. That was another reason for keeping the house and not moving into an apartment.

She had passed through Newton Village and now walked slowly up Strawberry Hill. By the time she reached the church, Mrs. McAlister was warm and she needed a rest. She opened the gate and glanced quickly at the stones in the churchyard. The door was open, the organ was playing softly.

That would be Lester Galli, the organist who taught music at the high school and often practiced here on Saturday mornings. With her coat draped over her arm, she walked slowly down the nave of the deserted church. The sunlight shone brilliantly through the windows on the left. Halfway down the aisle, she paused, slid carefully into the pew, sat down and laid her coat beside her. She crossed her hands in her lap and closed her eyes.

Ever since she had been a little girl she had daydreamed in church. It had seemed the easiest and most enjoyable way to sit quietly while the minister talked on and on. Now she let her mind go to memories. Memories of her husband, Dan, and how they had gone on picnics with their children, Elizabeth and James. Memories of James as a child.

As the time passed, the organ music got louder and faster, until it shook Mrs. McAlister from her dreams. Lester Galli was doing scales. Mrs. McAlister listened for a minute. It was time to be starting back. She would have a leisurely cup of tea in the kitchen with the noon sunlight streaming in the big window, and then she would take a warm bath.

There was a sound behind her.

"Mother." Surely she was still dreaming. "Don't turn around for a minute," the voice said. "Listen to me. It's Jim. Everything is all right, don't make a fuss. I don't want anyone to know I'm here."

Oh, my God, she thought. James. He's really here. James, my boy, my dear boy.

She started to turn.

"Please, Mother," he said. "Don't turn around for a minute. I'll come up there beside you. Is that all right?"

She couldn't speak. She was afraid that she would cry. But she must not make a fuss, if he didn't want her to.

"Mother," he said again. "Is it all right? I'll come up there."

She nodded. She could hear him moving. He was going to join her in the pew. She dug into her purse and got a handkerchief. She did not want to cry, but her throat felt tight.

Then she turned and saw him. He was coming into the pew, smiling. His eyes were sunk deep, and he did need a shave, and she was afraid she was going to cry.

He kissed her cheek. "Now don't cry," he whispered. "It's okay. I'm here, and it *is* me and everything is okay."

"I'm trying," she said. "I'm really trying not to cry." She was dabbing the handkerchief at her nose now, trying to suppress the little sniffling that persisted in forcing its way out. She was going to be all right. She looked at him and smiled. "How did you know to find me here?" she asked.

"You wrote to me about your Saturday walks. I took a chance. I thought you might be coming here. Can we talk for a minute?"

"Yes, of course," she said. "Why didn't you tell me? When did you come back? Are Tu-chan and the boys with you?"

"I'm just on a visit," he said.

The door at the back of the church opened and closed. He turned quickly. Mrs. McAlister didn't move, and after a moment she said, "What is it?"

"I think it was the minister," he said. "But he's gone."

"Are you afraid of being followed?"

"I'm not being followed." He turned to look at her again. "Don't worry."

"I just got your letter last week," she said. Her voice was trembling a little. "Why didn't you tell me you were coming?"

"I would have called you if I could. I have to be careful."

"I see," she was speaking softly. "Where are the children?"

"I have to go back."

"Why?" she said. "Why can't you bring them here? You can stay with me."

"But I have to go back," he said. "Listen, Mother, I can't stay long. There are some things I have to do. Some people from the Agency may try to find me and they may come here."

"To Newton?"

"Yes. If they do, I want you to tell them that I called you today, and that I am coming back. Tell them I'll be here Monday night, to stay with you. I want them to think I'm coming here so that they won't be looking for me anywhere else. Then I'll be able to finish up my work. When it's over I'll come to see you. Can I count on you, Mother?"

"If that's what you want." Lester Galli was playing another hymn, softly. She said, "Where are you staying, James? Can I reach you?"

Smiling, he reached out and took her hand. "You're not supposed to ask any questions," he said. "I don't want you to know where I'm staying. Then you won't have to lie if any-one asks you."

"Do you think they'll come and question me?"

"I think so. Just tell them I've talked to you and I'm com-ing back."

"When will I see you?"

"Later in the week." He patted her hand.

"If this works out, Mother, maybe we'll all be able to come back to the States soon. We may be visiting you next winter."

"All of you? Oh, James, that would be wonderful."

He was still holding her hand. "Can you tell them?" he said. "So they'll expect to find me here Monday night."

"Of course, darling."

He glanced around the church. The organ was still playing softly and the sunlight streamed in red and blue and green through the stained glass windows. There were threads of dust drifting in the air.

"You look beautiful, Mother," he said. "You're all right, aren't you? And how's my big sister?"

"Elizabeth's fine. We're all fine," she said. "Will I really see you next week, James?"

"Late in the week," he said. "Now I have to go. He leaned over and kissed her cheek.

She had to try hard again not to cry. "Take care of your-self, James," she said, looking down, "please."

"I will," he said and he left her.

Without turning around, Mrs. McAlister listened to his

footsteps. Lester Galli had the organ making little trills and they soon blotted out the fading steps. The door at the rear of the church opened and shut. He was gone.

She shut her eyes, drifting back into the comfort of her greatest dream. The house is big enough for all of us. Perhaps I will rent a cottage near Wilkins Lake. The boys should spend some time in the country like James did when he was young.

Mrs. McAlister blinked in the bright sun as she stepped out of the church. She looked all around slowly, up and down the street. There was no one in sight.

Chapter

19

IT was after dark when Eugene Cummings got home. He stopped his car in front of the open garage, closing his eyes and letting the tension drain from his body. The air was cold, and he could smell the coming rain. He turned off the headlights and then the engine. He was about to get out of the car when he saw the man come out of the dark interior of the garage. His head was down a little. In the darkness, Cummings couldn't make out the face. Then it was too late.

Cummings saw the gun and the square face and sunken eyes as the man yanked open the door and landed on the seat beside him. It had been a long time, but Cummings knew who it was.

"McAlister," he said. "For Chrissake, Jim." He started to put out his right hand.

The gun was coming up butt first.

Cummings tried to grab it, but the gun slammed past his hands. He tried to dodge it, but he couldn't. The gun came up fast and hit him squarely on the jaw. Suddenly pain was erupting in his head and behind his eyes.

"Sit still," McAlister said. With his left hand he checked for a gun, touching Cummings' pockets and his chest.

Cummings said, "What the hell is the point of this?"

"Now let's get out of here." McAlister stuck the gun in his belly.

Cummings' jaw throbbed. "Take the gun out of my side," he said.

"I'm going to tell you once, Gene. I'll kill you if you try anything."

"What are you doing? What's going on?"

Slowly McAlister moved back. "Just be quiet and drive," he said. "I want to talk to you."

The door behind McAlister was still open. Cummings glanced at the gun and at the door. If I can knock the gun aside and shove him out, I will be inside with the gun and he'll be out on his back.

McAlister had seen his eyes shift. Moving the gun slowly to his left hand, he reached behind himself and got the door handle with his right. Then he leaned forward and pulled the door closed.

"Now let's get out of here," he said.

"You didn't have to do all that."

"I'm not taking any chances, Gene. Now drive slowly. I want to get out of here."

"We can talk here," Cummings said. He took his handkerchief out of his breast pocket and held it against his throbbing jaw. There was no blood.

"Let's go." McAlister lifted the gun. Then he lowered his voice. "If you don't want to drive, Gene, I'll have to knock you out and do it myself."

Cummings turned the key and started the engine. He thought, if I slap the accelerator to the floor, the car will jump into the garage. That will spill him off balance. I used to be able to handle him. I could take the gun away and beat his head against the windshield, hard. But he is too alert now, too ready to shoot. It's too risky.

McAlister placed his right hand on the dashboard for support. "We've waited long enough," he said.

"All right," Cummings said. The headlights shone white on the garage, and the reflected beam lit up the car. He turned to look at McAlister.

There were lines in his face now and his eyes had sunk deeper. But it was the same thick hair, the same square face, and the same determination. McAlister hadn't changed.

Cummings pushed the reverse button and let the car slide slowly back without looking behind. "We could talk about it in the house," he said cautiously.

"Just drive," McAlister said.

"Martha would want you to come in."

"Not now, Gene."

Cummings shrugged. He stopped and pushed the drive button. He made a wide slow circle, tires crunching on the gravel. The wheel straightened out, and the headlights shot between the poplars. His jaw was throbbing. "You didn't have to hit me like that," he said.

"This is a nice place you've got here, Gene," McAlister said. "Did Martha pay for it?"

"It's Martha's place."

"You've done all right. When you get down to the road, you make a right turn."

"Where are we going?"

"We'll drive for a little while, Gene, and don't try anything," McAlister said. "I wouldn't want to kill you. But I will." He was holding the revolver against the back of the seat, muzzle pointed up.

Cummings slowed and turned onto the highway.

It was very dark out, and he couldn't see beyond the headlight beams or the sides of the road. He reeled down his window. The air was cold and heavy, probably close to rain.

McAlister was looking straight ahead now, and the gun was in his lap. It would be hard to reach.

Cummings drove slowly, following the course of the road and his thoughts. I have to get the gun away from him, but I will have to take him first. Take him with one blow. It will be difficult, but it can be done. Then I will shoot him with his own gun. Everybody is looking for him; it will be perfect.

Cummings spoke to McAlister. "How did you get here?"

"I came my own way."

"You should have called the Agency, Jim. We heard that you were here and that you might be working for them."

"I wanted to find something out. It should interest you."

Cummings could smell the rain. If it started soon, maybe it would help. The rain and the wipers would make noise, the road's curves would be wet and slippery.

McAlister said, "What's your title now, Gene?"

"I'm an assistant Deputy Director, Plans." He slowed a little on the long curve past the Logan Grocery Store with its dim spotlight falling on the two lonely gas pumps. "You should have contacted the Agency, Jim. We could use you again, especially now. We're trying to build the China section."

"I'll bet you could use me."

"What's the trouble, Jim?"

"I'm going back. That's the trouble."

"They can't make you go back."

"I've got a wife and two kids. I'm going back. That's where I live, Gene."

"Why didn't you call someone?"

"There isn't anyone I could trust."

"Christ, Jim, we were in school together. You could have called me. You could have come home with Martha."

"I thought I could trust Martha."

"Look, Jim, we can turn around and drive to the house. I can call Rynders. You remember Rynders, Isaac Rynders. He's Deputy Director of Plans now. We can talk to him. Maybe there's some way to get your family out."

"How is Rynders?"

"Same as ever. Eats aspirin like candy. What do you say, Jim?"

The first drops of rain had hit the windshield. McAlister said, "You couldn't get me out for twenty years. How are you going to get my family out now?"

"We can work something." Cummings smiled faintly. "The Agency owes you a lot, Jim. With all that back pay, you'll be a rich man. You've got a lot of seniority, too, and knowledge. You must have picked up a lot over there. You'll get a good spot."

"It won't work, Gene."

For a second they drove in silence. Raindrops covered the windshield. "All right," Cummings said. "What's eating you, Jim? Why are you back here? Why the gun?"

McAlister scratched his cheek. "I wanted to see Martha and you."

"You could have called me."

"That wouldn't have been very smart. Your friends are already too close."

"Are you working for them, Jim?"

"I thought maybe the Agency would be looking for me, but I didn't think you'd bring in the F.B.I."

"What's the job you're on, Jim?"

"I wanted to find out something, and I found out."

The road was twisting through low foothills. The wipers slapped from side to side and when a car approached from the opposite direction he had to squint into its headlights, and almost come to a stop until the car passed. The road wasn't very wide.

"You found what out?"

"I know about Korea, Gene. And I can prove it if I have to."

"What are you talking about?"

"Who put us down in China, Gene?"

"They had a lucky hit."

"There were two charges aboard. We found one, Gene.

We thought it was the only one, but we were wrong. There was another charge near the tail."

"Maybe the Chinese were right," Cummings said. "Maybe it was one of your boys."

"It wasn't. We knew that from the start. None of them could have rigged the charges or taken them aboard."

"We never found anyone at this end."

"I found someone, Gene. A couple of people saw you."

"Don't be an ass."

They drove for a second in silence. The wipers slapped back and forth.

"That's why I figure you'll help me," McAlister said.

"You've gone out of your mind." He glanced at McAlister. The gun was still pointing upward.

"I've been over there for nearly twenty years. It's a good story. If I have to, I'll go to the newspapers."

It was raining harder now. The road ahead curved gently.

"What are you talking about?"

"I'll call a few newspapers and the wire service. I'll tell them who I am—I think they'll figure it's a story. It should make quite a press conference."

"We'll close it up before you even get started."

"I don't think so. I'll tell them the plane really was bombed, and I'll tell them who put the explosives aboard. It'll finish you, Gene."

"I don't know where you get that idea."

"Peters saw you."

Cummings stared at him. "Peters. The crew chief. You've seen him?"

"I also talked to Borland. Your people just missed me."

"Peters made a mistake."

They were through the village. In a mile or so there was a sharp curve to the right. If he was going fast enough and if he braked hard enough, it would throw McAlister forward. Then he could hit the back of his neck with one hard slash, knock him out and shoot him.

"It will make a pretty story, Gene. After you put explosives aboard, and we went down, you married my wife."

"We'll deny it. Nobody will believe a man who is working for the Chinese."

McAlister shrugged. "I think we can make a little deal. I want a little help to even up for the years, Gene, and then we'll forget the whole thing."

McAlister was relaxed in the seat, the gun resting on his thigh. They were traveling fast, and the curve was just ahead. Cummings waited for another second. Then he touched the brakes.

With his left hand, he swung the wheel hard right. The car twisted and rocked, and went into a skid. Then, with both feet, he stamped on the brakes. The car bucked.

Cummings turned on the seat, lifting his right hand, fingers stiff, the edge of his palm like a knife blade. McAlister was forward off the seat, and the back of his neck was exposed. He was going to get him. He swung down hard, putting all his weight behind the blow.

But McAlister was moving, his shoulder turning. Cummings tried desperately to adjust the trajectory of his chopping hand. Clumsily, he hit McAlister's shoulder.

The car buckled to a stop, throwing them both forward.

Cummings felt the steering wheel ram into his chest, just as McAlister's right hand, and the gun, rose into his line of sight. He reached for the gun—an impossible prospect—and the butt tore along his chest, until McAlister drove it home up under his chin. It smashed his tongue to the roof of his mouth, and his throat constricted. He was choking. Cummings lurched toward McAlister, only to be pushed back. McAlister's wrist lay heavily across his throat like a bar.

He saw the gun an inch before his eyes, the round hole huge and black.

Cummings' mouth was open, gasping for air and straining for the word "No!" He grabbed McAlister's arm. The pressure let off a little. His first breath made an ugly guttural sound.

McAlister pulled the gun back and drove it hard into Cummings' face, tearing his jaw and cheek.

Then, spent, catching his breath, McAlister said, "Next time I'll shoot. Now let's get out of here."

Cummings' cheek felt warm and wet. He could smell the blood. Taking out his handkerchief, he touched it lightly. The pain burned through his brain. "Go to hell," he said.

"I want some information, Gene," McAlister said.

"Why should I? You're working for them."

McAlister waited for a minute. "I should kill you because of Korea, but that doesn't make any real difference now. I want you to get me something from the Agency. If you get it, I'll never be back. No one will ever know. If you don't, I'll ruin you." He sat back in the seat. "And if you try anything again, I'll kill you right here. Now start driving."

Cummings turned on the ignition. The headlights

dimmed for a second. Then the wipers started. Slowly the car moved along the edge of the road.

"Turn around when you can," McAlister said. "We can start back."

"What do you want, Jim?"

"A file from the Agency."

"I can't do that."

"I want the Agency file on a man named Kurlov, Felix Kurlov, also known as Klass, Felix Klass. I want to look at it."

"Why? Who's Klass?"

"He's supposed to be working for the Chinese. I want to find out a little more about him."

The road widened, and Cummings slowed and pulled onto the shoulder. It was still raining hard. "I'm going to turn around," he said.

"Slowly," McAlister said, bracing himself in the seat and pointing the gun in the direction of Cummings' heart.

Cummings turned the car around without incident and they headed back the way they had come. "What happens if I get it for you?" Cummings said.

"That's it. You won't hear from me again."

"What good does the file do you?"

"That's the job I took. They want me to check on him, and when I return I get a full pardon and citizenship. I've got a wife and children there. How about it, Gene?"

"I don't know."

"I want it tonight."

"It can't be done."

"Then tomorrow I tell my story."

"I'll try."

"That's not good enough, Gene. You can get it if you want to."

Cummings slowed as they approached West Village again. There were halos around the street lights.

"I can't do any better than try. We might not have a file on him."

"You've got one. He's a white Russian from China. If the Agency doesn't have a file, the F.B.I. sure as hell does."

"What are you going to do with it?"

"I told you. I'll look at it and give it back to you."

"You know what kind of a chance you're asking me to take." He intently watched the road which had begun to curve viciously, but he was thinking of McAlister. He could get the file, of course, and it would give him another crack at McAlister. He would be prepared next time. He said, "I could get it tomorrow."

"It has to be tonight."

Cummings glanced at him. McAlister was leaning all the way back in the seat, staring into the rain ahead. The gun rested on his lap. There was no expression on his square face.

"Believe me, Jim, you don't have to go back. We can talk to Rynders and set it up. We can get your family out."

"How about the file? Are you going to get it?"

"It will take me at least an hour. You can wait at my house—talk to Martha."

"That's nice of you, Gene, but we're going to do it my way. You get the file and take it home. I'll call you before midnight."

"You don't trust me."

"No," McAlister said, smiling faintly, "I don't trust you, Gene, and I don't want to kill you, either. I left my car on the road opposite your place. You can drop me there."

"I don't think I can be home by midnight."

"You can," McAlister said. He pushed himself farther into the corner. Now and then they smashed through a puddle. Up across a lawn McAlister could see the lights of a house glistening yellow in the rain.

Chapter

20

FOR the second time that night James McAlister drove west out of Washington on Route 82, past dark homes and farms and through silent villages. But because Route 82 is the main road to the mountains, every two or three miles, an all-night gas station with a diesel pump appears out of the darkness for the convenience of tourists and trucks alike.

Three hours earlier, McAlister had chosen one of these gas stations for his contact with Cummings. Then, a few minutes before midnight, he had called Cummings. Cummings had the file.

"Take Route 82 west until you go through a little village with a big sign called Fairfield," McAlister had told him.

"Stop at the first Esso station a mile north of the village. I'll be waiting for you."

He had set it up carefully because he knew that Cummings would kill him if he could make it look like an accident. If he didn't have the opportunity to kill him, Cummings might try anything, which is the trouble with any kind of blackmail. It makes people unreliable.

His headlights shone on the billboard: "You are entering Fairfield Village." He passed the sign, swung around a wide curve, and then entered the village. The tires splashed through a puddle left by the rain.

He would have to move quickly, Cummings would be desperate. He had figured that from the start, but it was possible that he had miscalculated, not been cautious enough. Cummings could bring in five or ten agents, or the F.B.I. or the local cops. But his instincts told him that Gene Cummings would run true to form. He would know that if he brought help, they might hear McAlister talk. Cummings' best chance was to kill James McAlister.

The road straightened out as it dropped into a wide, flat valley. The gas station was just ahead, ablaze with light on the right side of the road. It had two sets of gasoline pumps, side by side, and a diesel pump beyond. The asphalt apron was wide and clean. There was a neat station house and a service pit. A telephone booth glistened alongside the service pit, like an upright glass coffin. The outside telephone was one of the reasons for McAlister's choice. He could park on the road and have a good view of the station and the booth.

McAlister slowed and pulled up in front of the station house. The boy inside was reading, his feet up on the desk. He wore heavy shoes with red rubber soles. He looked up, as McAlister shoved open the door, but he didn't move.

"Evening," McAlister said. "Are you going to be open another thirty minutes or so?" It was hot inside.

"Yeah, sure, open all night, twenty-four hours a day."

The boy put his book down on the desk. "Every day of the year. You need something?"

"A man was supposed to meet me here, but I can't wait any longer." He took an envelope and a five dollar bill out of his breast pocket. "I'd like to leave him a note. Will you give it to him when he shows up?"

The boy stood up. He was a little fat and he needed a haircut. A thick shock of black hair fell across his forehead toward his heavy-lidded eyes. He was staring at the five dollar bill.

"Just a note, that's all?" he said.

"Just a note."

"Yeah, sure." The boy shrugged. "What's his name?"

"He'll ask for me," McAlister said, giving him the envelope with the bill. "My name's McAlister."

The boy shoved the bill into his pocket.

"He may not be by for a few minutes," McAlister said. "You won't forget?"

The boy was studying the envelope.

"It's a telephone number where he can reach me. It's worth five to me because I don't want you to forget."

"Okay, okay, I won't forget." He put the envelope on top of the desk. "Don't worry about it. A guy comes in here looking for a man named McAlister, I'll give him the note."

"Thanks," McAlister said. He turned and went back out into the refreshingly cool night. That kid kept his station house stifling.

He turned his car and drove back toward Fairfield until he could just see the lights of the gas station in the rear view mirror. Then he slowed and pulled onto the shoulder under a tree and settled back to wait. The night was still, except for the noise of a truck coming toward him, headlights bright, little yellow lights shining at the top corners of the trailer.

Beyond the road the valley spread out flat and dark and quiet. Shapes of an occasional house or a barn rose out of the landscape, barely discernible against a starless sky.

But the road was what required his attention. Cummings would come by here, and he must watch every car until he spotted him. McAlister took the .32 revolver out of his belt and spun the cylinder, checking that the safety was on.

His right knee was twitching, he was tense. Bright head-lights were approaching. He squinted and moved his leg to the right, but the knee kept on twitching.

He was in control. He had set it up so that he could watch Cummings to make sure he was alone and then to hit him when he did not expect it. He had to have a gun on him before Cummings even thought he had a chance.

The car flashed by in a gust of wind. He turned, watching its bright taillights. It did not stop.

Relax, it didn't do any good to be tense. If Cummings didn't come alone, he would not meet him. Perhaps he would drive back and wait for Cummings at his house. But Cummings was sure to come alone. Relax.

McAlister stretched out both legs, pushing himself back against the seat. But the right knee was still twitching. It was true. He was just too old for this kind of thing. But when he finished with Cummings, all the pieces would be in place and he would pick up Dr. Hermann, finish the job, and be done with it forever.

He left the .32 on the seat beside him. Two trucks were coming, one right behind the other. He watched them go by, spewing clouds of diesel smoke. There was no car behind them.

Eight cars passed, singly, with long spaces of timeless blackness in between. He hated waiting. Then a car went by, slowing a little. McAlister turned and saw the taillights flashing red. There was nothing else coming down the road.

He turned on the engine, and with his lights off, McAlister swung around on the road. The car had pulled up at the pumps. He turned on his headlights. If it was Cummings, he would get out of the car now, walk toward the telephone booth, call the number. But no one got out of the car.

The fat boy was standing at the rear of the car putting gas in the tank. McAlister drove by, slowly. There was a woman beside the man in the driver's seat.

McAlister looked in his rear view mirror. There was nothing else coming down Route 82. He had time to get back into position.

It was almost ten minutes before he saw the car coming slowly, its headlights on dim. His leg had stopped twitching. He had been wondering whether Cummings was going to come at all. The driver of the car was looking for something. McAlister leaned over, hiding his face from the light.

The car went by. McAlister sat up, turned on the engine and twisted in his seat. The rear lights flashed as the car slowed before the gas station.

McAlister looked back down the highway. There were no

cars following. Unless he had someone in the car with him, Cummings was alone.

His headlights off, McAlister slowly headed for the gas station. Cummings had parked near the station house. McAlister stopped in the highway. He saw Cummings come out of the house, pass his car, stop, and look all around. Then he went back and got into his car. He wasn't going to use the telephone. McAlister swore. He would have to follow him.

But instead of driving toward the exit, Cummings backed up slowly past the service pit to the telephone booth. He stopped, got out, and went into the booth.

McAlister had given him the number of a Washington department store. At this time of the night he wouldn't get any answer, but he would probably try the number at least twice.

There was still nothing coming down the highway. McAlister drove quickly toward the gas station, his headlights on high so they would be blinding. He turned into the station, driving rapidly, the gun secure in his right hand. He headed for the far side of the telephone booth. The booth would be between the two cars, and it would be next to McAlister's window. He hit the brakes and came to a hard stop. The gun barrel shone out the window.

Gene Cummings was holding the telephone to his ear. He saw the gun pointing at him through the window. He hung up the telephone.

With his left foot, McAlister kicked the parking brake. He pushed the neutral shift button and opened the car door. Slowly, with the gun still aimed at Cummings, he started to get out of the car.

Cummings' eyes were following the muzzle of the revolver.

McAlister moved out of the car, the gun raised, its safety off.

"Come on out," McAlister said. He stood at the doorless side of the booth.

Cummings was wearing a clean tan raincoat. His face was pale and unearthly in the artificial light. His lips were the color of liver. He kept both his hands away from his body, and walked out of the booth.

"I was calling you," Cummings said.

"I know. Turn around and keep your hands out to the sides where I can see them."

"I brought you the file."

"Good. Now turn around. Keep your hands out."

"I could have sent some people."

"I'm going to frisk you."

He reached out with his left hand and grabbed the back of Cummings' raincoat at the collar. Then, stepping backward, he pulled it down hard, twisting his fist so that Cummings fell backward off balance, until McAlister caught him with the coat at the small of his back. He pushed Cummings away, turning him. Cummings staggered back against the doorless side of the telephone booth, his arms pulled back and down by his coat.

Then McAlister saw the edge of the shoulder harness. Stepping in close, he jammed the gun into Cummings' belly, hard.

Cummings doubled up, grunting and cursing.

Quickly, McAlister fished the automatic out of the shoulder holster. He tossed it to the ground, with a clatter. He touched Cummings' hips, his pockets. He wasn't carrying another gun.

He stepped back. "Where's the file, Gene? I'm in a hurry." He started toward Cummings with the gun aimed at his stomach. He would drive it all the way to his backbone.

Cummings stepped backward awkwardly, rounding the corner of the booth and stumbling inside. "In the car," he said.

"Stay in the booth." Watching Cummings, McAlister picked up the gun from the ground and jammed it into his coat pocket. Then he went to Cummings' car. The door on the front passenger side was open. He glanced onto the seat and saw the envelope.

"You're not going to take it," Cummings said. "You can't take it."

"I'm taking it."

"I signed out for it. You were just going to look at it." He stepped out of the booth.

"Stay there," McAlister said, lifting the gun. Cummings stopped. "I'll get it back to you."

"You can't do that. They've got my signature. Somebody may want it."

"You can get around it, Gene."

He backed until he hit the side of the car, next to the open door. Reaching back with his left hand, he groped over the seat until his fingers touched the envelope. He brought it out and stepped away from the car.

He got the file out of the manila envelope using only his left hand. It was a dark brown dossier with a long index number, beginning with the letters BH. Resting it on his gun hand, he opened it and, catching the name Klass on the first item, the tissue of a memo, he closed the file.

"Why don't you look at it right now," Cummings said, cocking his elbows out and shrugging his shoulder. "You don't have to take it."

"I'll get it back to you. It won't be missed," McAlister said.

"Jim, maybe there's a way. We could work it out so you can do the job for them, give them the information they want, and then go back. We'll figure out how we can get you and your family out. We can go talk to Rynders."

"I'll get in touch with you," McAlister said.

"You can't take that file."

"You'll get it back in a day or so. Nobody will know."

"What if something goes wrong?"

"Nothing will." McAlister walked around the telephone booth to his car. He had left the door open, and the engine was still running. He tossed the file onto the seat and got in, still aiming the gun at Cummings.

With his left hand he released the parking brake, pushed the reverse button. The gun pointed out the window. Slowly he backed up until he could swing around the rear of Cummings' car. Then he went past the gas pumps and out of the corner of his eye he saw the boy reading in the station house. He sped out onto the empty highway, heading for the mountains. He snapped on the radio. He could turn around anywhere.

Chapter  21

THE agent's name was Michael Renfrew. "Renfrew," Mrs. McAlister said carefully. "Michael Renfrew?" She had opened the door just wide enough to peer out at him.

"That's right, Mrs. McAlister," he said, smiling. He had his foot against the bottom of the open door. She couldn't slam it on him.

Michael Renfrew was an accountant by training. He had a pleasant face and large ears, and he was known at the Boston office for asking questions as if they were pleasantries. He and his partner, Maretti, had found the house at 229 Brixon Road without difficulty. Mrs. McAlister reportedly lived alone, and there was no car in the garage, and the street was deserted.

Maretti had stayed in the car parked in front of the house in case there was any trouble or anyone came out. If Renfrew didn't show up in twenty minutes, he would come into the house.

He took out his wallet and opened it to show her the shield. "From the Federal Bureau of Investigation," he said.

"Oh," she said, staring at it. "From the F.B.I." She peered up into his face. Her white hair was arranged in tight curls about her head. "It's Sunday," she said. "I just got back from church."

"I hate to bother you, Mrs. McAlister," Renfrew said, smiling again, "but I'd like to talk with you for a few minutes."

"About what?"

"It's about your son," Renfrew said.

"That's what I thought," she said.

"It won't take very long."

She stepped back, opening the door all the way. "I suppose you may as well come in."

He looked through the hallway into the living room. It was always possible McAlister was in the house, and he would be armed. Whatever he had been before, he was now an agent working for the Communists. And Renfrew had his orders: locate him. Call in all the help necessary.

"You could have called," she was protesting.

"I'm sorry. There wasn't time," he said, returning his attention to her.

She swung the door closed. "It's just that I live alone. I like to know who's coming," she said. "I was making some tea. Would you like a cup of tea, Mr. Redthrew."

"Renfrew," he said, laughing a little as he corrected his name.

"I always have a cup early in the afternoon," she continued. "I'll fix you coffee if you prefer."

"A cup of tea would be fine."

"You put your raincoat in the closet," she said, pulling open the closet door. "I'll get the tea."

The closet was neat and empty. A bunch of metal hangers, a woman's cloth coat, a raincoat, and a jacket hung one behind the other. Against the side wall someone had left a man's raincoat, brown and dirty and old. Renfrew hung up his coat. Then he stepped into the closet and quickly dug into the raincoat pockets. Nothing.

He took off his hat. He was six feet tall, but he had to stand on his toes to see the top of the shelf. There was a small box and nothing else. It was empty. Putting his hat on the shelf, he stepped back and closed the closet door. If McAlister were staying in the house, he wasn't using the front closet.

Renfrew was admiring the window-box flowers in the living room when the kitchen door opened. She was carrying a small tray crowded with white china. "I'm very particular about my tea," she said, as she set the tea set down on the large table in front of the couch. "I always have a cup when I get home from church.

"How do you like your tea, Mr. Redthrew, with lemon or milk?"

He sat down on the end of the couch. "It's Renfrew," he said. "A little milk would be fine if you don't mind."

"Oh, I am sorry." She peered at him. "I had your name wrong. Renfrew, not Redthrew. I do apologize."

"It's all right," he said.

She poured the tea and handed him the cup. "Now," she said, "Mr. Red . . . Renfrew, why do you come to see me about James after all these years?"

"Just a routine check."

"Routine," she said. "Oh, come now." She glanced at him over the rim of her cup. "I hardly think it's routine."

Renfrew watched her, still stirring his tea. She sat on the edge of the cushion across the table from him, straight and prim, holding the cup and saucer in her left hand just above her knees. She was neither as old nor as addled as she seemed.

"Years ago," she said, "when I tried to get the government or you people to do something about James, nobody would do anything."

She sipped her tea. "It's been many, many years, Mr. Renfrew, and in all those years nobody has made any routine checks, as you call it. Not once in all those years. So it hardly seems routine to me."

"I understand your feelings," he said. "Well, Mrs. McAlister, we've had reports that your son may be back in the United States. We wondered if you had heard from him."

"That's hardly routine," she said, pressing the issue and peering at him in an incongruous grandmotherly way.

Renfrew smiled. "We make these kinds of calls all the time."

"I'm an old lady," she said, "but I don't think I'm a fool. Why do you think he's here?"

"We just want to know if you've heard from him."

"We write, of course," she said. "James writes me every week. But I think you have it all mixed up, Mr. Redthrew. You see, I wrote the State Department people, just as they asked me to, and told them I was going to visit James again this summer. That's probably where the rumor started. And that's why they've sent you. But you can tell them I shall go no matter what they do. Unless, of course, they put me in jail."

"Mrs. McAlister . . ."

"And my lawyer told me that they wouldn't dare to stop me." She put her cup back on the tray.

Renfrew pulled at his right ear. "I'm sorry," he said. "I hadn't heard anything about that. But we did have some reports that your son had returned to the United States. And if he has, Mrs. McAlister, it's very important we talk with him, for his own sake." He finished the cup of tea. "Perhaps he has tried to reach you?"

"Well, I don't know," she said. She stood up. "I did get a telephone call, but I dismissed it as a crank. Oh, my goodness. If James were here, in this country, it might not have been a crank call."

That's it, Renfrew thought. "You got a crank call today?" he asked.

"It was yesterday. That's the day I take my walk, and it was just after I got back. I just dismissed it as a crank, but now I don't know."

"You didn't recognize the voice?"

"Oh, no, it wasn't James. I would recognize his voice."

"What did he say, Mrs. McAlister?"

"Now, let me see," she said, looking intently off into space. "He said he was calling about James." She looked at Renfrew. "I was rather surprised, and I asked who it was. He said that his name didn't make any difference and that he was calling for James and would I be home on Monday night."

She smiled. "That seemed a rather silly question, and so I asked him again who he was, and he said that he couldn't tell me but he was calling for James." She waited.

"He sounds rather mysterious," Renfrew said pleasantly. "What else did he have to say?"

"Well," she said, "he told me that I should be home tomorrow night, Monday night, and then he hung up."

"It could be possible. You never know." He pulled his ear again and he thought, That's it. He's in the States and he called or had someone call to make sure she was going to be home. He's going to be here late Monday night. We can pick him up. But if he calls again, she might warn him.

He said, "Are you going to be home tomorrow night, Mrs. McAlister, just in case?"

She said, "Do you think I should be?"

"It probably wouldn't do any harm," he said. He took out his wallet and extracted a card. It had his name and the Boston office address and telephone number. "This is my card. We'd appreciate it if you'd let us know if you hear from him."

"It would be wonderful if it really is James," she said. "Do you really think it could be?"

"It could be," he said. "But if you have any trouble with cranks, Mrs. McAlister, don't hesitate to call us. Ask for me."

"That's very kind of you," she said.

Renfrew smiled and stood up. "Thanks for the tea," he said as he walked down the hallway to the closet. "I'm sorry to have troubled you." He got his hat and held his coat over his arm.

"You will let me know if you hear anything about James, Mr. Redthrew?"

"Renfrew," he said. "If I find out anything, of course."

"I don't know what's wrong with me. I can't seem to get your name right. I'm sorry."

"It's all right," he said. "Goodbye, Mrs. McAlister."

Renfrew felt the wind in his face as he crossed the lawn. Maretti was sitting in the car, watching the house. Apparently no one had come out. He had done pretty well. McAlister was coming here, and they could get him. As soon as he reported in, Washington would take over.

Maretti had moved into the driver's seat. Renfrew pulled open the door and slid in. The air was laced with cigarette smoke.

"How was it?" Maretti asked, as he reached down to turn the ignition key. His cigarette bobbed up and down in his mouth when he spoke.

"The old lady's kind of addled, but he's going to be here Monday night. Someone called and told her he'd be here. She didn't recognize the voice, but it was probably him. She thought it was a crank."

Maretti smiled. "Beautiful," he said. "We'll pick him up like a chicken."

"Pluck him, you mean," Renfrew corrected. "The expression is to pluck him like a chicken. Washington will be happy."

"They had top priority on it," Maretti said, pulling away from the curb. "Maybe one of us should set up a watch. He might come early."

"We'll let Washington decide," Renfrew said. "They're going to want to run the show." He looked out the window. The wind was tossing the trees.

"That was pretty good work," Maretti said, "getting it out of her when she didn't even believe it herself."

"It took a while," Renfrew said. "Apparently she doesn't even know he's working for them. I left her my card. She's an old lady, and I thought maybe I was taking advantage of her." He smiled.

"Just pumping her?"

"No," he said. "No. But she said she'd call us if she heard from him. It doesn't seem right, his mother going to tip us." He smiled again.

Maretti chuckled, shaking his head and coughing on the smoke from his cigarette.

Chapter

22

DR. Karl Hermann fought the wind all the way across the dark campus. His head bent forward and one hand held his hat on his head. He stepped around the corner of the Administration Building, away from the lighted sidewalk and into the wind. A gust sent the end of his scarf flying. He was headed for the Faculty Club. Since Traude's death, he had eaten supper late at the club almost every night including Sunday.

He peered into the darkness, looking for the carriage lamp that hung beside the club door. But it was hard to see without his glasses which he had tucked into his vest pocket because of the wind. Then the lamp shone out, a dull orange yellow. He turned into the walk, still holding his hat and listening to the wind rustle in the hedge. He grabbed the brass door handle and shoved the door open.

Inside, it was quiet and dim. He blinked. The light was fuzzy around the big chandelier. Across the black-and-white marble floor he could just barely make out the wide glass case that was part of the counter. He dug under his coat to get the steel-rimmed glasses from his vest. When he put them on, the glasses slipped into a worn notch in his nose. The room was less full than usual, probably because of the hour. He had stayed late at the office, expecting the man to call. He had said he would call before the end of the week, but he had not called.

Dr. Hermann walked into the coat room and unwound the scarf from his neck. It was one of the long scarfs Traude had bought him. She had liked him to wear scarfs. He pushed the wooden coat hangers aside, and they rattled. It was warm in here and quiet. He could hear the wind battering against the little window. It had been blowing all evening, a real spring wind like the wind in the mountains, cold and fresh and gusty.

He remembered how he used to stand on the hillside near the cottage and feel the same kind of wind on his face. He would look across the valley at the little houses, the square green fields, and the village down below. He could see as far as the white mountains across the valley in the distance.

He took off his hat and put it on the shelf. He brushed back his white hair and then he got out of his raincoat and hung it up. They said when you get old you start remembering childhood, but he wasn't that old and he was a long way from senility. Yet ever since Traude died, he had these fleeting memories of his parents and their little house in the mountains. It was the sound and the smells of spring that reminded him.

He reached under his suitcoat and took hold of the points of his vest and pulled them down, flattening the vest. He stuck out his jaw, wiggling it and stretching out his long neck to make his collar fit comfortably, and then he left the cloakroom and crossed the marble floor to the glass case counter.

There were two desks side by side in the area behind the counter. The club steward, Mr. Victor, was adding up some items on a little electric adding machine.

Dr. Hermann cleared his throat. "Good evening, Mr. Victor," he said. "Rather windy out tonight."

"Real spring winds," the steward said. He had a perpetual suntan, and he spoke with a lilting English accent. He had come from somewhere in the Caribbean.

"You saved me my Sunday newspaper?"

Mr. Victor looked up. "Oh," he said, realizing for the first time who it was. "Evening, Professor. I have a message for you, I do believe."

"For me?" Dr. Hermann was surprised.

Mr. Victor reached out to get the pink message pad from the adjoining desk. He looked at it. "Just called, not ten minutes ago, Professor. A Mr. Hamill. Apparently he called your office and the operator switched him over here."

"Is that all, Mr. Victor? Did he leave any message for me?"

"I told him you generally arrive by this time, Professor. He said he would call back in a few minutes."

"You'll let me know when he calls?"

"Yes, I will." He made a little flourish with his pencil on the pad, tossed it onto the desk, pulled a newspaper out of one of the drawers, and handed it to Dr. Hermann.

"Thank you, Mr. Victor," Dr. Hermann said. "You'll let me know if that fellow calls?"

"Yes, sir, most assuredly. Don't you worry about it. You have an enjoyable dinner, sir."

Dr. Hermann nodded and turned, holding the thick newspaper under his arm. There was a little elevator just back of the staircase but he preferred to walk. He trudged slowly up the wide staircase, one step after the other toward the dining room.

Hamill had finally called. Perhaps now they would get on with it. It was more than two years since he had first talked with Felix Klass, and he was rather tired of waiting. It would be good to get it done. As Klass had said, it was very dangerous and if they caught him they would surely kill him. But he and Traude had known that from the beginning. Traude had worked with the Party years ago, and knowing they would one day die anyway, they had promised each other to do something to make the dying worthwhile. He was going to keep that promise.

The dining room was large with orange draperies pulled over the west windows. The reddish wall lamps shone the color of dull roses on the polished wooden floor. A few people were still having dinner on the far side of the room.

The waiter saw Dr. Hermann and came to escort him to his usual table in the corner. "Evening, Professor," he said, pulling out the chair.

Dr. Hermann sat down. "Good evening, Jack," he said,

"how's your family?" He put the newspaper on the next chair.

"Fine, thank you, Professor, just fine. One martini, dry?"

"Yes, and I'd better look at the menu."

As soon as Dr. Hermann opened the front section of the newspaper his eye caught a story on the front page below the centerfold. He read quickly:

DISARM TALKS CONTINUE

Soviet and American diplomats announced today that top level disarmament talks have been scheduled to continue through next Wednesday and probably through the weekend.

Announcement of the continuation of the talks was made in a joint communiqué, issued by the Secretary of State and Premier S. I. Menshikov who personally heads the Soviet Mission which has been in Washington for a week.

Dr. Hermann looked up from the paper. That meant they had time if it was to be done while the mission was in Washington. Perhaps that explained why Klass had not called with the final orders. Felix Klass had insisted they wait for the disarmament talks, and now it seemed they were going to continue for another week at least. Klass and their man, Hamill, must know what's going on.

He found the column again.

The brief communiqué insisted progress had been as good as could be expected, although all parties concerned now agree considerable technical work can be carried out by subcommittees and technicians.

Dr. Hermann skipped a few paragraphs.

The announcement took official Washington by surprise. The talks have been held in strict secrecy, and diplomatic sources offered differing interpretations of the increased schedule. White Paper diplomats, who have strongly supported the recent State Department paper on anti-missile systems and disarmament, insisted that the continuation indicates negotiations have progressed more rapidly than originally anticipated.

However, other Washington experts, who had held out little hope for the talks, believed the diplomats had deadlocked and looked to subcommittees and technicians to find some way out.

Dr. Hermann looked across the room, thinking: governments, and most people, prefer the excitement and the same old tensions because they are not really afraid. They will never achieve disarmament unless reality shocks them, unless they themselves feel destruction. They will go on forever with their conferences, negotiations, discussions, until it is too late, until darkness comes.

Traude had said that, especially after the A2-100 project. People arm in fear. They will only disarm in fear. He had been consultant to the Disarmament Agency project at Rochester, and they had developed the A2-100. They had proved that with refinements the A2-100 would be as foolproof as any detection device could be. But the Pentagon, the State Department, and the politicians would not listen.

It was during the summer of that same year that they had seen Jagens in Hamburg. In the early days when the Nazi rowdies had swaggered in the streets, they had marched with Richard Jagens, and they had known his pretty young wife, Hilde, and their two children. Traude had been secretary of the Jagens group. They had left in time, but Jagens stayed. He had spent the war years in Russia, and then, he married again in Hamburg. In his little house on Liderstrasse there was a picture of Hilde and the two children he had lost.

Jagens had seen it coming again, too, with the American airfields in Germany and the missiles and the nuclear warheads and the growing tensions. But that first summer they had just been old friends. It wasn't until the year after that they talked about what they could do to promote disarmament. Then, when they got back from their summer vacation, Felix Klass had come to visit them.

Dr. Hermann wondered if Richard Jagens knew what they were going to do. It did not seem that he could. Jagens was now a rather bitter, low-ranking professor at the Polytechnic Institute where Dr. Hermann had earned his doctorate. And yet he was aware of things, he traveled, he knew people in Hamburg. He had even sent them to visit some friends in Italy. Also, somehow, he had learned of Traude's death and he had sent a note, unsigned.

The waiter brought his martini and put the menu on the side of the table. Dr. Hermann put down the newspaper, realizing that he had been holding it up like a shield while staring out the window.

"Thank you," he said. The martini was ice cold, sharp, and bitter.

It was Jagens and then Klass who had advised him to accept the State University's offer to transfer here. The University wanted his reputation at the new division, and, as they said in the journal, Dr. Karl Hermann was a recognized pioneer in electronic and computer control technologies. He held a hundred and twenty-three patents, and he was a consultant in the design and production of nuclear weapon controls. Dr. Hermann had been at Rochester ever since he came to the United States, and he had not wanted to move. But the University had been good to him, and even Traude had agreed that he should accept the transfer.

Dr. Hermann finished half the martini and was just about to order his supper when the waiter told him there was a telephone call for him. He could take it at one of the telephones in the foyer.

He went out quickly and stood for a second looking at the telephones. He could hear laughter coming from the bar. The telephones were on a shelf on the wall, affording no privacy, and this was their man Hamill calling. For a minute he considered going downstairs to one of the booths. But he was alone in the foyer, and he would take the chance that no one would disturb him. He picked up one of the telephones.

"Yes, sir?" It was the girl on the club switchboard.

"This is Karl Hermann," he said. "You have a telephone call for me?"

"Yes, Dr. Hermann. One minute, please." The telephone hummed and crackled.

Dr. Hermann said, "Hello."

"Karl Hermann?"

"This is Karl Hermann speaking. Who is this, please?"

"Hamill," he said. "Sorry to bother you, but I wanted to check in. I tried to get you earlier."

"Yes," he said.

"Is everything all right?"

"Yes, everything is fine. You were going to let me know when you would meet with me."

"I've still got a few things to work out, but it will be to-morrow. I'll pick you up at your house."

"At what time, Mr. Hamill?"

"Ten o'clock in the morning."

"I shall be ready for you. Mr. Hamill, have you heard from Felix Klass?"

"Klass? Not since the contact."

"He was supposed to call me. Does he know of your plans?"

"I don't know," McAlister said. "I haven't talked to him. You have everything ready, Dr. Hermann?"

Dr. Hermann was nodding his affirmation. "My things have been ready for some time."

"I'll see you tomorrow," Hamill said. "Goodbye, Doctor."

"Goodbye." Dr. Hermann hung up. He had been really rather foolish to worry. Their man had called just as he had said he would. And Felix Klass would call or contact him, too, as planned. Klass did not like telephones. A number of times in the past he had waited in his car in front of the house.

Dr. Hermann reached under his suitcoat and pulled down the points of his vest, flattening it. The young men were laughing in the bar. Soon, he thought, soon. In another day it would all be over. Nodding to himself, he walked back into the dining room.

Chapter

23

A jet whined louder and louder and then took off screaming, somewhere on the other side of the terminal. Clutching his briefcase, McAlister looked out into the late afternoon sunlight at the parking lot just across the road. He had left the rented car there four days ago.

A tan Cadillac drifted past him and stopped, holding up the steady stream of cars. McAlister stepped behind it and crossed the pavement. A roar shuddered through him. Against the scattered rain clouds and the blue sky, a jet was climbing fast, racing its own plume of smoke and glittering in the sun. It left a smell of fuel in the air.

As he walked down the sidewalk toward the parking lot, McAlister thought about the old man's two suitcases. Uneasy, he had insisted upon going with him to the baggage carousel. But the only things out of the ordinary were last season's skiing posters still in the advertising frames on the wall.

The suitcases were a lot heavier than if they had been packed with clothes, so McAlister had carried them himself to the escalator and the busy waiting area. Then he had made Dr. Hermann comfortable in a red plush chair, leaving the suitcases on the floor beside him. When he had explained that he would be a few minutes getting the car, the old man had smiled and bobbed his head. He still held the book he had been reading on the plane.

McAlister went through a break in the guardrail. The lot was arranged in double rows. His car was in the middle, in row four. The General had the license plate number so he should be able to find it.

McAlister found the car and unlocked the front door. It had been baking in the sun, and the air was hot. He opened the window, put the briefcase in the back seat, and then he waited a minute, to let the car cool a bit. A car slowly entered at the other side of the lot and swung into a parking place. There was no sign of the General or anyone else.

McAlister got into the car, leaving the door open. He found the key and put it in the ignition. Now he would just have to wait. He glanced at his watch. The General was about five minutes late.

Finally he heard steps falling on the pavement. Turning, he saw him step between the cars. McAlister reached over and pushed open the far door.

"It's good to see you, my boy, good to see you."

He came in sideways, wearing a hat but no overcoat, his face pink and damp from the heat.

"You're a little late," McAlister said.

"Someone came out of the terminal right behind you, my boy, and I wanted to let him drive away first. I presume everything has gone well."

"He's waiting in the terminal. He still expects to talk with Klass."

"I tried to tell him about Klass a few days ago. It didn't do any good. He does not know that Klass is dead."

"Klass was going to give him some final instructions."

"That is your problem now," the General said.

"What about the tickets?"

"Ah, yes, the tickets. You are on a direct flight from here to Montreal, both of you. I'm afraid you must take care of the old man that far."

"I figured that. I won't make it unless he does."

"The names are on the tickets, and you don't need passports so there should be no problem. But, just in case, we have supplied passports under the ticket names." He pulled a white envelope from his inside jacket pocket. "The old man has his own passport under his name and you have one under Hamill. You go on different airplanes from Montreal."

"How long is the layover?"

"An hour for the old man and a little more than that for you. It is safer, my boy, if you put him on his airplane first, and then you can be sure . . ."

"All right," McAlister said. He took the envelope. It was dirty with fingerprints. Inside there were tickets and a green passport.

"How about money?" the General asked.

"I have enough, and I'll take care of the old man. Where's he going?"

"Brussels. We will take care of him from there."

"What about me?" He was looking for a ticket. It was Scandinavian Air Lines.

"Oslo," the General said. "I didn't have much time and our people there are convenient." He smiled faintly, showing the little teeth. "They will ask about the time, my boy, and they can take care of you."

McAlister put the tickets back inside the envelope and tucked it inside his coat pocket, behind the wallet. "We have to be here by eight o'clock in the morning. It's going to be close."

"You can go right on the airplane, my boy. You are confirmed." He tossed his cigarette out the window. "It is hot here like the South. I spent years in the South, and this is the end for me, too. I am going back."

"When?"

"As soon as you are finished. The YMCA will miss me. I have been here too many years."

"You'll be a hero."

"I am never the hero, my boy. You are the man who has made it possible."

"I checked Klass." He turned and reached into the back and got the briefcase. He lifted it carefully and brought it over the seat and put it on his lap. "I have something for you, General." He snapped the catchlocks, opened it and reached inside. The file was on top of a dirty shirt. He took it out and handed it to the General. "It's the file on Klass," he said.

"Whose file?" His little eyes were staring.

"I'm not sure," McAlister said, "but I got it through the C.I.A. The man who got it for me isn't going to tell anyone. I want you to get it back to them."

"I see," the General said. He was getting another cigarette. "What does it show?"

"Nothing," McAlister said. "Not a damn thing. They had everything about him except the essentials."

"Why do you want me to get it back to them?"

"We can never use that source, and they should know your organization can get a folder out of their files. It will shake them."

"You have other reasons as well," the General said. "Personal reasons." He got his cigarette lit. "It was a dangerous thing to do." He puffed on the cigarette. "They know you are here."

"But not why, General. I set it up so they're looking for me in Connecticut. By the time they understand, it will be too late."

"You should have consulted me."

"I told you, no case officer. Now I'd better get back to the old man."

The General's beady eyes still stared at him. He was breathing hard. "I hope that you have not made a mistake," he said. "For all of us, McAlister, and for your family." He put on his hat and started to get out.

"Good luck," he said, patting the hat. "I can do nothing more for you now."

"I'll make it," McAlister said.

The General shut the door and squeezed his way between two cars. He walked slowly almost all the way across the lot to a green Ford. He unlocked the door and got inside, ignoring the heat. He went through the file. McAlister was right. There was nothing of any importance about Felix Klass. He had come to the United States from Brazil, but they did not know that he had been raised in China before he went to Brazil, and they did not know that Felix Klass had once been Frederick Kurlov. They did not even know that he was dead.

When he finished with it, he put the file in his suitcase. Then he put the suitcase on the pavement and locked up the car. A car could sit here a long while before anyone found it.

The General felt weary as he carried the suitcase across the hot lot, up the stairs and into the terminal. It was busy, and he had almost an hour before his flight to New York. Just enough time to get something to eat and relax.

There had been so many things to do, the tickets and arrangements, and then cleaning out everything at the apartment, making sure that no one would ask questions for at least a week; making excuses about why he could not help with the fund drive, closing his savings account, paying bills and the last installment on the big television set. He had even left a false forwarding address at the post office so the mail would not pile up.

The General sat down at the counter of the terminal coffee shop and ordered two cheeseburgers and a cup of coffee. He had become so used to his frantic life that it was going to be hard, after almost seven years, to spend all the days in the country wandering in the back wood near the stream. But there were grandchildren now, and he would build a little house there, right by the water, so that they could all live together. He would read in the afternoon and in the evening work on the stamps and maybe some of the children would be interested in them. He imagined himself sitting in the little house at a table with the sound of the water outside, and maybe one of the older children, Mitka or Natasha, who would be almost eighteen by now, helping him with the stamps.

He was looking forward to the flight because he would get a chance to sleep. When he got to New York he would stay at the hotel right there at the airport and be ready for the early flight in the morning.

The General slept all the way on the airplane, his head on a pillow jammed between the seat and the window, and he didn't wake up until his ears began to hurt as they were coming down.

He called up the hotel from the terminal while he was waiting for his suitcase. They confirmed his reservation. He would get the evening newspaper, and then watch a television program in the air conditioned room. When he saw the suitcase fall from the entrance on to the conveyor belt, he shouldered his way gently through the crowd and picked it up as it went past.

He headed for the street. He would have to get a taxicab and that was always a nuisance, especially at night.

There was a cluster of people at the curb. Perhaps if he walked farther down the sidewalk he could catch a taxi there. The suitcase was heavy, and it slowed him down.

Someone touched his arm. "Excuse me, sir."

"What?" he said, turning as he walked. It was a young man.

He had something in his hand, his open wallet, a shield. It glistened faintly, and then he flipped it closed. "Federal Bureau of Investigation," he said.

"I beg your pardon," the General said. There was another one to his left. Two of them.

"We'd like to talk to you, Mr. Knowles, if you don't mind, sir."

"Why me?" he said. How did they know his name?

One young man had taken his left arm. "The car's right over here," he said, directing him.

"What's going on?" the General protested. They were walking too fast.

"If you'll just get in the car, please, sir, we'd like to talk with you."

A black sedan was at the curb.

For a fleeting second he wondered if there was any way to get rid of the suitcase, but he knew that it was hopeless. Then he saw the other man, in the shadows, coming forward.

"I don't understand," the General said.

"Just get in the car, Mr. Knowles," the young man said.

The third man was coming closer. The light was almost milky in his thick glasses. "We've been waiting for you," he said cheerfully. "Just get in the car, Mr. Knowles, and everything will be all right."

Someone had taken his suitcase. The car door was open. One of the men went in ahead of him. They knew what they were doing. The other one took his arm and half-lifted him into the car.

"I don't understand what is going on," he said, genuinely annoyed.

The one with thick glasses got in the front, and slammed the door after himself. A few people were watching them from the sidewalk. "You will," he said.

"Let's go," the man in front said. "We may not have much time."

Chapter  24

"WE'VE waited an hour," McAlister said. "Klass has been sick. He isn't going to make it."

"We will wait a few minutes more," the old man said, turning to McAlister. In the lamplight his glasses were like mirrors. "If he can, he will be here."

The old man had been standing at the window with his hands clasped behind his back, looking out at the darkness and the valley.

"It's dangerous for us to wait," McAlister said.

"I know," the old man said. "That Mr. Knowles talked with Felix. If he can, Felix will be here."

"He had better get here pretty soon," McAlister said. "We should start by midnight."

McAlister walked past the fireplace. With only one light

in the living room, he could hardly make out Hallee's face in the photograph on the mantel. But the silver frame glowed.

The old man looked at his wristwatch. "In twenty minutes it will be midnight. If he does not get here by then, we will go."

"All right," McAlister said, crossing the room again. It was absurd to wait. Yet he didn't want to tell the old man that Klass was dead. Not now. When it was all over, he would tell him. "I'll load the car," he said.

Without turning on the light, he went into the kitchen where they had put the suitcases. The old man had taken out the two boxes and the battery case. The black instrument boxes resembled old radios in steel cases, but they had too many dials and switches. The old man had riveted handles to the ends for carrying.

McAlister bent down and got hold of the handles on the larger of the two and stood up. It was more than two feet long, a foot high, and very heavy.

Walking sideways, he went out the screen door and down the steps. The dog came out of nowhere to sniff at him. "All right, Rufus," he said, "just get the hell out of the way." The dog leaned against him, and McAlister shoved him with his knee.

He put the case down in the driveway behind the car and opened the trunk. Then he lifted the case, put it inside, and went back into the house for the smaller one. By the time he got back into the living room he was breathing heavily.

The old man was still standing at the picture window with his hands clasped behind his back.

"We're all ready," McAlister said. "We ought to leave now."

"We should finish long before dawn?" It was a question.

"How long will it take you?"

"Perhaps an hour," he said, nodding. "Unless we have difficulty locating the cable."

"Then we better get started." McAlister wasn't taking any chances. You never knew what unexpected obstacles might present themselves.

Dr. Hermann walked to the desk and sat down. "I think it is better that we wait for Felix. We had agreed he would be here."

"If he's sick he can't get here."

"I should wait for him."

"All right," McAlister said, watching him. "All right, Dr. Hermann. He isn't going to be here. He may even be dead."

The old man rocked forward a little over the desk. He turned his head, sticking it forward like a turtle, peering. "Dead?"

"He had a heart attack last week. Even if he isn't dead, he's not going to be up for a long while."

"Mr. Knowles did not tell me that."

"I don't think he knew how severe it was."

"Perhaps he was lying to me."

"He didn't want to upset you."

"No," the old man said, "no. The Russian did not want Felix here."

"He was working with him. He's been helping me."

"Felix did not trust them, Mr. Hamill, because if they knew the truth they would stop us."

"Why would they stop us?"

The old man was nodding. "The missile is programmed to a target in the Soviet Union. It would be very difficult for me to change the program."

"But it's supposed to come down in that valley where you live, in New York."

"That is what the Russians think."

"Does Peking know about this?"

"I am sure they do," the old man said. "It was what we discussed from the first, but it was necessary to talk about re-targeting."

"You realize what will happen?"

"Yes," the old man said, nodding. "Of course. It will force the Soviet Union and the United States to agree on disarmament. It is the only way to insure that they do."

McAlister stood still. They hadn't told him this. He was supposed to get Hermann out here, and let the old man do the work. But the missile was supposed to go down in that valley. The Russians thought it was going to come down in the States, too, and yet they had been afraid. That is why they had sent the General. They must have seen the possibility.

He said, "You launch it at the target, it could start a war . . . everything."

"No," the Professor said, shaking his head. "No. It will not start anything. The Russians know that we are here, and their Mr. Knowles is here, and they know we are launching the missile."

"Maybe you're wrong about Klass. Maybe he didn't want it this way."

255

"If they changed anything, Klass or one of his people would have to tell me. He is not here." He stood up. "We will go, Mr. Hamill. You have the equipment in the car?"

"It's all packed."

"We will go then," the old man said. He walked quickly to the kitchen doorway and disappeared. The screen door slammed.

It took McAlister a few minutes to go through the house. He turned out the lights, closed the windows, locked the kitchen door from the inside and went out on the front porch.

The dog was waiting for him. It was a warm night and that peaceful silence had settled over the valley. Only a few lights shone out of the darkness. With the .32 in the pocket of his jacket, and the jacket slung over his shoulder, McAlister pulled the front door shut and locked it. He had promised Ann he would take care of the dog.

"Come on, Rufus," he said. "Let's go."

As he walked around the house, the gun in the pocket of his jacket bounced against his back.

The old man was sitting in the rear seat of the car, waiting.

Chapter

25

THE light woke Ann. Holding the covers, she sat up and looked at the alarm clock. It was ten minutes after twelve. Incongruously, the room was lit like daylight, and she could hear voices in the street. A car door slammed. Then the light went away, and the room went black.

She threw back the sheet, got out of bed, and dressed quickly in her slippers and her robe. Standing to the side of the window, she looked out between the edges of the shade and the frame. There were four cars parked in front of the house. On the sidewalk, men were standing in groups.

One man walked up the driveway and another approached the front door of the house. The doorbell rang once. They were surrounding the house.

Ann had already started down the steps when the doorbell

rang again. Mrs. McAlister stood in the front hall, wrapped in a light blue robe, her white head cocked a little to one side as she stared in bewilderment at the back of the front door.

Ann called, "It's all right, Judith, I'm here. I think it's the police." She hurried down the stairs.

A few strands of Mrs. McAlister's white hair had fallen down the back of her neck. "At this time of the night?" she asked.

"It's all right," Ann said. "We can let them in, but we won't tell them anything."

"I told you about the man from the F.B.I.," Mrs. McAlister said. "I knew they'd come—James wanted them to come—but I didn't think they'd come in the middle of the night like this."

The doorbell rang again.

"You stay there, Judith," Ann said. "I'll let them in."

"As far as we're concerned he's still over there, is that right?"

"That's right," Ann said, patting her arm.

The man who had been ringing the doorbell pounded with his fist.

Ann let go of Mrs. McAlister's arm and pulled open the door.

The man was big with the bright light behind him, and he seemed to be leaning forward, about to topple over.

"Yes," Ann said, "yes, what is it?"

"From the Federal Government," he said. "Sorry to bother you at this time of the night."

She looked up at his face, at the tense mouth. She was not

sure, but she thought that it was Eugene Cummings from the Agency, the one who had married McAlister's wife.

"We're looking for someone," he said. "May I come in?"

Behind him a man moved across the lawn. One of the spotlights went on and then off again. There wasn't any reason for him to come in.

Then he noticed Mrs. McAlister standing in the background shadows. He called to her. "Mrs. McAlister," he said, too loudly. "Mrs. McAlister, how are you? It's Gene Cummings."

He stepped past Ann and held out his hand.

Mrs. McAlister stared at him, her mouth open a little. She said, "What are you doing here at this time of the night? What do you want?"

She didn't take the hand he offered.

"We're looking for Jim, Mrs. McAlister. We understood he might be here, and it's very important that we find him. We want to help him."

"He's not here," Ann said brusquely.

"Have you heard from Jim, Mrs. McAlister?" Cummings asked.

She looked from him to Ann and back to him. She pursed her lips. "He writes to me every few weeks," she said.

"But have you seen him here? We understood he was going to visit you."

"James back? In the United States?"

"That's what we were told," Cummings said. "Have you seen him?"

Mrs. McAlister shook her head.

Cummings turned to Ann. "How about you?"

"Even if I had," she said slowly, "I would not tell you."

"I see," he said. "We've met before, haven't we?" He crossed his arms on his chest.

"A long time ago," she said. "My name is Mrs. Ann Learson." She started to shove the front door closed. "Mr. Cummings, you and your men have awakened us in the middle of the night and you have disturbed the whole neighborhood. We have told you James is not here. Now if you don't mind, we'd like to get back to bed."

"Mrs. Lee. The pilot's wife." Now he remembered her well.

"Widow. My name is Learson. Now if you don't mind . . ."

"What are you doing here, Mrs. Lee?" He stood with his arms folded looking down at her; he had no intention of moving.

"I'm visiting. We've been friends for many years."

"Have you talked with Jim, Mrs. Lee?"

"Don't be absurd."

Turning back to Mrs. McAlister, Cummings said, "It's very important that we talk to Jim. We understood he was coming here tonight. When do you expect him?"

She puckered her lips in thought. "Gene Cummings," she said, shaking her head. "I can remember when you and James were in school together. But how many times did I come to see you in Washington, how many times? And you never did a thing to get him out of there. You never even tried."

"We did our best."

"You could have gotten him out if you had wanted to."

"Jim and I were friends, good friends. We did everything we could."

"I don't believe you," she said firmly.

"For his own good, Mrs. McAlister, it's important that I talk with him. You *are* expecting him tonight . . . ?"

"No," she said, shaking her head.

"That's not what you told the F.B.I."

Mrs. McAlister took Ann's arm. She smiled. "I didn't tell the F.B.I. man anything." Then, turning, she started down the hall toward the stairs. Ann followed her.

"Now," she said, "I would like to go back to bed if you don't mind." Cummings didn't move. "If you don't mind, Gene Cummings, this is my house. Good night."

The hall was silent for a moment.

Cummings spoke deliberately. "I'll have to search the house."

"You need a warrant," Ann said.

"If that's what you want, O.K. But we'll have to turn on the spotlights and watch the house until I get the proper papers."

Mrs. McAlister called down from the hall upstairs, "What is he saying?"

"If we don't let him search the house, they'll turn on the spotlights. I suppose we might as well let them search."

"I hope it won't take too long," Mrs. McAlister said softly. She dabbed at her eyes with a handkerchief. Tears glistened on her cheeks. Frustration and rage.

"After you finish, Gene Cummings," she called, "I'll

thank you to get out of my home. You get out and stay out."
Then she turned and disappeared into the darkness of the upstairs hall.

"How long will it take?" Ann asked.

"Maybe fifteen minutes."

"He's not here," she said. "I can promise you that."

"I'll get one of the boys to look around downstairs," he
said. "You can show me upstairs, but first I'd like to make a
telephone call. May I use the telephone?"

"You don't really have to ask, do you?"

"You're not being much help."

"I don't mean to help."

"Where's the telephone?"

"In the living room," she said, gesturing down the hall.

He had his wallet open, and flipping up a page of the pad
inside it, he picked up the telephone and dialed.

"This is Eugene Cummings," he said. "Let me have Plans
duty officer, please."

He looked at Ann, then back at his pad, and then his eyes
examined the little room. "Hello, Jim," he said. "Cummings
here. We've drawn a blank so far, but we're still looking.
Any developments?"

There was a pause and then Cummings straightened. He
slapped his wallet closed. "Wait a minute," he said. "Slow
down." His face changed as he listened. "You're sure?" He
listened for a moment more and then he smiled.

"Okay. You talked to Missile Defense Command?"

He waited and said, "Rynders is right. They shouldn't
take any chances. Shoot on sight. You tell Rynders that's
what I said."

He dropped the telephone into the cradle, leaving his hand resting on it for a second.

"Son-of-a-bitch," he said softly. "He just might do it." Buttoning the top button of his raincoat, he turned and started out of the room.

"What is it?" Ann said. "What's happening?"

He looked at her, startled—he had forgotten she was there. "He's been staying at your place, hasn't he? Near Sterling."

She didn't answer.

"And he sent you away tonight. Do you know why?" He stepped closer to her. "Because he is over here to launch a missile, and he's trying to do it tonight. He's got an expert working for him. We picked up one of the people in Soviet Intelligence we've been watching."

"But that doesn't make any sense," she said, unable to disguise the confusion and the fear in her voice.

Cummings smiled. "McAlister is working for the Communists. He's trying to set off a missile. A missile carrying bombs."

"No," she said. "No, he couldn't."

"Maybe he already has. And he couldn't have done it without your help." Cummings went down the hall and pulled open the front door. Once outside, he waved his arm to the two men stationed on the lawn.

"Let's go," he said. An engine started. Two men came down the driveway. A small gathering of people had assembled on the sidewalk, and from among the crowd a flashlight shone on the house. A radio crackled.

"Ann?" It came from behind her. Mrs. McAlister was

waiting at the top of the stairs. "Ann," she called again. "What happened? Did they find James?"

"Yes," Ann said, standing at the front doorway. But she hadn't spoken loudly enough and her hand covered her mouth.

"What did he say?" Mrs. McAlister was coming slowly down the stairs.

Except for the crackle of the radio and the soft sound of the engines, the four cars at the curb were rather quiet. Then the headlights snapped on, and the first one started smoothly and slowly away. There was nothing to do now except wait until morning.

Chapter

26

McALISTER stopped digging for the first time when the hole was almost three feet deep. He was sweating and his arms ached. He leaned on the shovel and looked at Dr. Hermann.

"I'm down at least a yard," he said.

"You're getting close to the cable. You should rest for a minute," Dr. Hermann said.

McAlister looked at the skinny old white-haired man and he thought, That is the one thing I don't need now. I need to keep going and finish it. I have to be done with it and get away from here.

They had left the car on the valley road just north of the woods. They would be going away from the missile site and the launch control headquarters. To make it look good he had rolled out the sparetire and positioned it against the outside fender. And he had left the jack lying on the ground nearby.

It was carrying the cases that had started him sweating. By the time he had lugged the second case into the woods, the old man was wandering along the side of the road in his open raincoat, peering at the dial of an oversized compass, trying to locate the cable. There was enough current going through the service cable to set up a field.

"What time is it?" McAlister asked.

The old man stuck his left arm out of his sleeve. "It is almost one o'clock," he said. "We have enough time. You are close to the cable now."

"I'm down pretty far." The hole was the size of a small grave. His shirt was wet with sweat. It clung to him.

"You must be careful not to strike it."

"I'll be careful," McAlister said. "You had better get the equipment ready."

His right hand was moist with sweat and it slid along the long smooth handle of the shovel. He was digging carefully. He positioned the shovel and leaned his weight on it, pushing it into the soil. Then he worked it loose, lifted and heaved.

The old man was on his knees in the road, working on the boxes.

Gently, McAlister pushed the shovel blade in at an angle. He hit something only a few inches down. If it wasn't a rock, it definitely would be the cable. He flattened the blade, tossing the earth out of the hole. Then, letting the shovel fall to the ground, he crouched and reached down with his right hand.

He shoved aside the loose dirt. With his fingers, he could feel something hard and smooth. It was plastic pipe. The old man had said they ran the cables in plastic pipe.

"You found it?" the old man asked.

"I think so. Let me get around it. The pipe is pretty hard."

"It is vinyl."

"What?"

"It is polyvinyl chloride pipe. You must expose about a foot."

"I've got my fingers under it. It's pretty thick."

"That's it."

McAlister dug through the loose dirt with both hands, pushing it to one side. When he could run his hand under a foot of pipe, he stopped and stood up. Putting both hands on the edge of the hole, he scrambled out. He stood up and rubbed the back of his neck. The old man and the dog were both watching him. He said, "It's not supposed to be this hot this time of year."

"We will be finished soon," the old man said. "Just a little while now." He was holding some round clamps and a tool with a cutting wheel.

"There is pressure in the pipe," he said. "That is how they know if there is a break. So we must clamp it before I can open the pipe."

"Won't they get a drop in pressure anyway?"

"But it will take time, and I only need a few minutes."

"All right," McAlister said. He looked up at the sky. It was still black and starless, and there was no moon. The rain will cool things, he thought, and it won't slow us down. We can be out of here in only a few minutes. We will drive straight north out of the valley, and pick up the highway. That thing will have finished its flight and its destruction long before we drive out from under the rain.

Dr. Hermann was still working on his knees in front of the cases. McAlister could see the switches on the control panel. It did not look like a very modern piece of equipment. The old man turned each of the switches twice, forward and back, making soft snaps and nodding his head.

It will come down over there, McAlister thought, as he watched. It will kill thousands of men and women and kids, and not just the few hundred people who live in that valley.

"Is it going to work?" he asked.

The old man turned the last switch forward and back. "This is the control console." He started to stand but it was an effort for him. McAlister put his hand under his right arm and helped him up.

"Someone's coming," the old man said, pointing with the tool through the woods toward the valley road.

McAlister turned. Headlights. They were shining softly as if through a fog, coming slowly north along the road. "It's just a car," he said.

"You didn't damage the cable?"

"I didn't damage anything. It's just a car."

"It is the first car we've seen slowing down. He's going to turn in."

The lights were high in the trees and still far away.

"What do we do if he comes in here?" the old man wanted to know.

"We stop him, but he's not coming in here." The lights flickered slowly through the trees.

If he had hit the cable pipe too hard or if they had tripped something, the only people who would be coming here would be guards from the launch control center. The .32 in the pocket of his jacket could take care of that.

The lights were moving very slowly, like a wall, as the car crept toward the service road.

"He'll have to stop to take down the chain," McAlister said. "If he turns in, you get out of the way." He got the gun out of his jacket.

"You must have hit the cable," the old man said. "You must have broken the pipe. That is the only thing that would have brought them."

"I didn't hit anything," McAlister said. He clicked off the safety button on the gun. "It could be a routine check. You better get off the road." He stepped into the trees.

When they came down the road they would see the cases and they would stop. He would have to move through the woods quickly so he would be behind their car.

The wall of light was just south of the entrance to the service road. For a while it didn't move, long enough for someone to take down the chain.

When the light started moving again, McAlister expected it to sweep through the woods on its turn and come flashing down the road toward them.

But it moved slowly, flickering through the trees. Then, speeding up, it swept past the entrance to the service road. It was not turning in.

The old man spoke first. "Why did he stop?"

"I don't know." McAlister wiped his face with the wet handkerchief. "It's too damn hot, and we're both jumpy. What time is it?"

The old man looked at his wristwatch again, holding it close to his face. "Just after one o'clock," he said. "We still have plenty of time."

He took off his raincoat, laying it down on the road. He was wearing a blue shirt and an old jacket that looked as if it were made of denim. He started to bend down to pick up the smaller case.

"I'll get it," McAlister said. He lifted the smaller case by the handles. It was attached by a cable to the other case.

"You will have to be careful of that cable," Dr. Hermann said.

McAlister carried it slowly to the edge of the hole. The cable was plenty long enough. He put it down on the ground.

There were loose wires neatly coiled and taped hanging out the back. They ended in clips, each a different color. "You've got five or six wires there," he said. "Why so many?"

Dr. Hermann had taken off his glasses. He got a tissue from his pocket and started slowly polishing them.

With the glasses, he pointed at the wires. "Two of the lines must carry the main signal. In the control cable, they are run from separate control panels at the launch headquarters. The two men on duty must turn their switches simultaneously.

"The green line," he said, "is the master inhibit. The launch control center down the valley is only one of ten that control missiles in this group. When one of the control centers fires its missiles, any one of the others can inhibit. So we must block out the inhibit line.

"The pink lines are monitors. They carry feedback from the missile. The feedback signals must be retransmitted over the firing lines. That is to prevent accidental firing or tampering."

"Do you have to connect all of them?"

"Five," the old man said, nodding. "Five."

Dr. Hermann put his glasses on again and sat down on the edge of the hole. Swinging his legs in first, he lowered himself into the hole and started to examine the cable.

He said, "It will take me a little while to get ready. Everything must be prepared before I clamp the pipe."

"All right," McAlister said. "I'll be back in a few minutes." He stepped over the connecting cable. He wanted to look at the missile site. It was only a little way to the edge of the woods. Beyond them, the road was gray-white. Fifty feet out it went under the fence, then across flat ground until it ended at the edge of the silo.

Dr. Hermann would have it ready in a few minutes, he thought. They planned it this way, the people in Bow String Alley knew from the beginning—everyone knew, except me and the Russians. The dog pushed his head against his leg. McAlister scratched him behind the ears. "It's going to be all right," he said.

271

As he walked back into the woods he could hear the old man working in the hole like an animal. He stopped nearby. The old man was bent over. He had put clamps loosely around the pipe. "How's it coming?" McAlister asked.

"I am almost ready." Dr. Hermann stood up and began to climb out of the hole. McAlister offered his hand to help.

"We will test the equipment," he said. "Then we will be ready."

"How long will it take after that?"

"I must clamp the line, cut into the cable and make the attachments. Perhaps a minute, no more than two."

"What do you want me to do?"

"I will check the instruments," the old man said, walking toward the other box, "and you must remain ready to turn them on when I tell you."

Dr. Hermann got down on his knees again and began turning the dial. A faint orange light glowed through the perforations. The old man worked for a minute, and then he said, "Now, Mr. Hamill, you will have to turn this when I tell you. That is all you have to do." With his hand on a dial, he demonstrated. Turning it to the right produced a series of clicks. "You turn it just this way," he said. "Not too fast."

"All right," McAlister said. "I can do that. What about the other switches?"

"Everything else is programmed," Dr. Hermann said. "You should not touch anything else. Would you like to try this a few times?"

McAlister crouched and tried it twice. A faint hum emanated from the box, and a few of the rows of small orange lights on its front blinked off and on.

"What do the lights mean?"

"If there is a failure, I can find it. You do not have to worry about them."

McAlister stood up. He was still sweating.

"Now," the old man said, "I will have to use the flashlight for a few minutes. You turn the dial when I tell you."

"Then what happens?"

"The concrete cap will blow aside. It will take the missile between three and four seconds to get out of the silo."

"I'm ready," McAlister said. "Then we're going to have to get out of here fast. We may have to run."

Dr. Hermann smiled faintly. "I'm an old man," he said, nodding, "and I cannot run very fast. But we will worry about that later."

McAlister crouched by the case, the little lights winking at random. He thought. It will take less than half an hour to get to its target. It will be morning there, people getting up, children dressing, the streets clean in the early light. Some people in heavy coats may already be outside, moving in the streets, in the cold.

The light from Dr. Hermann's flashlight flooded up out of the hole, making him look like a gravedigger, bent over, throwing shadows as he moved.

"Do you want me to hold that light?" McAlister asked, getting up.

"No," the old man said. "It is only a few seconds. Do not move."

The light made McAlister nervous. It could attract attention. But Dr. Hermann was working fast, fastening the wires. Then suddenly he dove down. The flashlight went out, and they were in darkness again.

"Now," the old man said as he climbed out of the hole on all fours. "Now, Mr. Hamill. You can turn the dial, please. Slowly, do not go too fast."

McAlister was watching Dr. Hermann coming toward him like a dog, as if he could not get up. "Now," Dr. Hermann repeated, urgency in his voice. But he was still crawling. "You must turn it now," he yelled.

McAlister reached for the dial, but the old man had come up alongside him, still on his knees. Reaching out, his hand shaking, Dr. Hermann grabbed the dial and turned it.

McAlister listened to the progressive clicks. The little lights blinked quietly on and off, and nothing happened. He stood up.

The old man had finished and was sitting quietly, his full attention focused on the missile site. His glasses balanced crookedly on his nose and his mouth had dropped.

McAlister waited, but there was only blackness. Then he started walking toward the edge of the woods.

The two explosions came fast, one after the other, like gunshots. The cement silo cap blew up and away like the huge top of a coffee can popped by a firecracker, and disintegrated in white smoke.

McAlister could hear the missile sounding like escaping air, and then buzzing loudly like a million bees. The ground was trembling, but nothing came out of the hole. It wasn't going to launch.

The sound turned to a roar. Orange appeared in the white smoke. He crouched.

The ground shook. The noise filled the sky, deafeningly loud.

As if in slow motion, the missile rose. The white nose of the warhead, and then the flames burst out. Intense heat spread into the air, scorching his face. He crouched lower, slapping his hands over his cheeks trying to get away from it and still watch.

In the roaring heat the missile waited, poised for an instant. Then it shot up, the flames flashing and leaping. It was going. McAlister peered out through his hands into the furnace.

It went up, thundering, its flame like an arrow. Then the missile turned, still climbing, and seemed to slope at an angle into the black sky over the ridge. For an instant the flame went white, a sun hidden in the clouds, and disappeared.

McAlister's face was still hot. His hair was singed. And the air smelled like burning tar. Suddenly, he remembered the old man and he turned, still half blinded by the brightness in his eyes as he scanned the nearby terrain.

The old man had come up behind him. He was staring at the sky, open-mouthed, his arms hanging limp at his sides.

"We've got to get out of here," McAlister said. His voice sounded loud; he was shouting.

"What?" The old man was dazed.

"Let's get moving," McAlister said, touching his arm. "Through the woods. To the car."

"There are headlights already," Dr. Hermann said. He

nodded and slowly pointed back toward the valley road. "I saw them before."

McAlister couldn't see any lights, but he heard something. A siren. "Come on," he said. He pulled Dr. Hermann's arm and started walking.

"You can leave me," he replied.

"They'll be coming soon. We can make it. Just walk with me." He got the old man moving, holding his arm, tugging him, urging him to move a little faster with each step.

They went back along the road, and then McAlister pointed toward the woods, the way they had come. He had to keep the old man ahead of him, or he would fall too far behind. The siren was coming up the valley road. When he looked back through the trees, he could see headlights. "Can you run?"

"I'll try," the old man said, starting to jog, stiff-legged. He stumbled through the underbrush. McAlister grabbed his arm, holding him up until they were out of the trees. Now he could see across the field. The car would be waiting there.

"You go ahead," the old man said. "Go ahead."

"Just hold on," McAlister said. "We're almost there."

The siren was screaming louder. He saw the lights, faint at first, as they ran, struggling and stumbling. And then there was light all over the meadow, pushing shadows out from under the trees. He glanced back. There were at least three cars turning into the access road.

In this light anyone could see them running, unless they went flat. But that was impossible. The old man was panting, each step requiring increased effort. McAlister could see their car with the trunk up. If they could make it to the edge of the field, to the barbed wire fenceposts. . . .

Someone shouted from far away. The old man tripped. McAlister put his arm around him to keep him moving. Then he saw the bright light sweeping down the road. It was a spotlight.

He could hear the engines and the men yelling.

"I can't. Let me go," Dr. Hermann protested. But McAlister dragged him on.

The old man stumbled again. This time McAlister couldn't hold him and they went down. The spotlight was sweeping over the meadow. After it passed he started to pull Dr. Hermann to his feet.

"It's no good. I can't go any farther."

McAlister leaned over. "Take hold of my neck."

The siren had stopped. They were playing the spotlight in the woods now. And the light reflected in the old man's glasses.

"We're getting out," McAlister said. He put one arm under the old man's legs and the other around his back. "Get hold of me," he said.

"It's too late." His body slumped, wet and limp.

McAlister stood up, lifting his heavy weight. He started toward the car. The spotlight came on again. It was only fifty yards to the road.

Someone yelled. The light was bright over everything. They had been seen.

McAlister kept running. Another light came on. "Stand right there." The voice did not sound like a man's voice but like a machine—a bull horn.

McAlister couldn't stop now. It was only a little way. Soon he would be at the car, and he would escape the lights.

"Stop!" the voice called again.

McAlister tried to prompt his legs to run faster. Then something banged and cracked beside him. He could see the car just ahead now. Just a few yards more.

Something hit him in the arm. He was going down, Dr. Hermann hanging in his arms. More shots rang out.

The old man jumped like a doll, like a doll he used to have when he was a boy. It would walk if you set it on the ground when you wound it up. But if you held it, it jumped and twitched and jumped.

McAlister tried to stop himself from falling but he couldn't. The light was in the grass as he landed, and the old man was mumbling something.

Another man's voice said, "I think the old guy's dead."

There was pain in his arm and his shoulder and his chest. Even with his eyes closed, he could see the bright light. When he opened them, he saw the face staring down at him. "We're giving you a shot. You'll be all right."

McAlister tried to tell the man about Dr. Hermann, about the doll, but the pain swept up out of his chest. He heard his own voice screaming, and then nothing.

Chapter

27

HE had been drifting pleasantly, listening to a soft, steady vibration somewhere. When his eyes opened he saw a woman. And, on the other side, a man wearing thick glasses stood gazing down at him. He looked familiar.

"How do you feel?" the man asked him.

"It's all . . ." The words were out of reach.

"It's Isaac Rynders," the man said. "It's going to be all right."

"Tu-chan." Longing, fear, and confusion clotted in his chest.

"Yes, I know. You took a chance. But it's all right. We got the missile before it went anywhere, satellite warning system."

"The missile?" McAlister summoned his strength to listen to the man. What had he said?

"We got it down. It didn't go anywhere. It's all right."

"Tu-chan," was all he could say. Tears fell from his eyes.

"Listen to me," Rynders said. "We picked up Knowles. We persuaded him to talk. We were ready for the launch. Now we're going to make a trade. We'll have Tu-chan and your boys over here, but it will take a few days. The Russians have to do it. . . ."

"No," McAlister pleaded.

"You had better leave him now, sir," the nurse said. "He needs rest."

Rynders nodded and turned back to McAlister. "It's going to be all right," he said. "We know about Cummings, and we are going to take care of you."

But McAlister's answer was "No." He did not understand, and he was afraid. A sadness overwhelmed him. His eyes closed, letting the darkness cover him as he wept, "Tu-chan."

Isaac Rynders' head was splitting. He followed the nurse out of the room and down the hall. The pain was throbbing and pushing against his eyes.

Seeing McAlister cry shouldn't bother him so much.

Far away down the corridor, he saw Maxwell coming from the elevators. He had told him to meet him here. Rynders took a small bottle of aspirin out of his pocket and unscrewed the cap. He put four of the pills into his mouth and chewed them.

"How's he doing?" Maxwell asked as he approached.

"He's all right," Rynders said.

"Mr. Lucas wanted me to tell you that the President wants

to congratulate the Agency. He said the accidental firing has given further impetus to the talks—something like that."

"How about the Russians?"

"They want to talk about the arrangements," Maxwell said. "I told them we'll keep Knowles on ice for a week. After that, we start asking questions, and we'll squeeze him dry."

Rynders' right eye was hurting worse now.

"The Director thinks you are going to a lot of unnecessary trouble," Maxwell said.

"We owe McAlister something."

"The Director said the Agency doesn't owe him anything."

Rynders walked toward the elevators. He rubbed his eye with his fingertips, knowing he shouldn't. At least the pain would go away for a few seconds.

Maxwell was right behind him.

"So we get his family over here," Maxwell was saying, "and he'll be all right. He could have been killed."

"That's not even what he wants," Rynders said. "He wants to go back over there."

"Hell, we can't do that."

"I know," Rynders said and he pushed the down button.